Angel Fire

ISBN: 9781706761372
©™®

Patricia Carragon
9/11/22

0

To my family and friends,
thoughts, and dreams.

Special thanks to Cindy Hochman
of "100 Proof" Copyediting Services.

"Words have no power to impress the mind without the exquisite horror of their reality."
—Edgar Allan Poe

Chapter 1

Sarah
(2001)

Sarah Kahn couldn't find her slippers. A cold sweat dampened her brow. Her thoughts wrestled with questions. Her intuition compelled her to write what she saw; otherwise, something bad might happen.

Like slumber sheep, her dreams demanded a recount. She wondered if this was a premeditated joke. Was stress the culprit? Why was she upset over the child's threats? She had never even met her outside of her dreams. However, Sarah, a sucker for superstition, believed, without understanding why, that this kid wanted these chapters written, and Sarah wanted to write a novel.

She pulled her long mousy-brown hair back into a ponytail before activating her Mac. She created a folder called *The Allie Chronicles* and placed a new Word document inside of it. She bit her tongue as the story moved across the screen.

A girl named Allie skipped across the playground. The sky was a perfect shade of blue, like her blue mini-dress trimmed in white lace. The sun was shining—a perfect setting designed for children's stories, but this wasn't a perfect story.

She skipped toward the monkey bars, singing. Her song had no title. She had complete ownership of the playground. Like

a chimpanzee, Princess Allie swung from one bar to another,
grunting. Joy radiated throughout her kingdom, and her world
was perfect now; no nasty bullies or grown-ups around to spoil
it. As she swung closer to the sky, she forgot how pretty clouds
could sometimes turn ugly and chase Mr. Sunshine away. When
she saw a dark blur move through the azalea bushes, she stopped
singing. Was the blur a dog, a cat, or a rabbit? Allie had to
investigate.

Sarah stopped typing. She recalled yesterday's dream and a few she had been having over the past weeks. They involved Allie's mother, and Allie was the narrator. Sarah's fingers moved back into action.

Allie became a loner due to circumstances. She was born
Alexandra Katherine in New York City, a mistake conceived by
deception between two feckless people. Back in the late '50s, her
mother, Siobhan O'Neal, an auburn-haired Bronx girl, was
looking for a rich hitch at Steinberger's Department Store.
Allie's father, Charles Hudson, a wealthy middle-aged schmatte
merchant of Jewish descent, was peddling his wares to the girls
on the sales floor. He had accidentally planted a few seeds, and
those seeds had often sprouted on the doorsteps of orphanages.

Allie's story had originally been written more than fifty
years ago in a journal kept by Siobhan O'Neal. Siobhan had
wanted to be a writer, but her lack of motivation, coupled with
low self-esteem, kept her out of City College. Much to her
parents' dismay, she took a job as a salesgirl at Steinberger's
and pursued her writing at night.

Shamed by her Catholic family for her reckless sin,
Siobhan moved out of the Bronx apartment off Fordham Road.
She spent the rest of her pregnancy on her own, her abortion
expenses covered by the reluctant Charles.

In a dingy office at Goldstein's Mercantile Warehouse
down on West 54th Street, she handed $600 to the stocky matron
who claimed that Dr. Samuels was on the way. But the doctor
never showed up. The matron looked at her watch and said,
"Sorry, honey, these things happen," and then packed her bag,
pocketed the money, and departed. After the woman left, Siobhan
paced the hallway. The November chill crept through the broken
window. She didn't know what to do.

An albino mouse scooted past the stairwell. Siobhan's
mother believed that the souls of murdered people lived in mice.
Seeing the ghostly mouse frightened Siobhan, as she feared that
this was a bad omen.

She thought about the journal kept in a drawer by her
bedside. Each page became an evolving story of her life, as if a
fortuneteller were speaking through her fingers—meeting
Charles Hudson, the wealthy merchant who had knocked her up
and left her to pace these cold hallways in this godforsaken
warehouse, waiting for the abortion that would never be. And
she would die giving birth to this child, Alexandra, and the child
would be born cursed. Something terrified her about this
journal, but she needed to write another entry each night.
Writing was her addiction and only fulfillment in life.

Yet she refused to cry, too proud to admit her loss. She slowly walked down the stairs, accompanied by echoes from her shoes. Her faithful loafers took her to the subway and to her walk-up on West 115th Street. She immediately called Charles but, as usual, he wasn't available.

Seven months later, she was admitted to the emergency ward at Mother Cabrini Hospital. Avoiding her pleas for money, Charles conveniently took a trip to Chicago. Due to complications caused by fibroids and internal bleeding, the Caesarean delivery proved fatal. From the baby's neck the doctors and nurses removed the tight noose made from her mother's umbilical cord. They thought it was a miracle that this baby had survived.

Deirdre Smith, one of the nurses, kept her promise to Siobhan, recalling her request as she was being wheeled into the delivery room: "If it's a boy, call him John Michael; a girl, Alexandra Katherine." Siobhan had had a premonition that she would not live to see her child.

The motherless newborn screamed like a banshee. Deirdre made the sign of the cross before swaddling the bathed infant in a blanket.

The O'Neals buried their daughter at Woodlawn Cemetery in the Bronx and forgave her. Little Alexandra was transported to Elisabeth Styles' Home for Children in Manhattan and wasn't forgiven. The family wanted no part of the demon child with fiery hair. As far as they were concerned, this wailing creature had killed their daughter. Their motto was: "Keep her out of sight and mind, and let God take care of the rest."

After saving the document, Sarah's fingers paused. She sat motionless, watching the screensaver flip from one scene to another—kittens, ranging from domestic shorthairs to exotic. Cute, but they couldn't appease her irritability. With the coming of sunrise, the strident tweets of the birds kept her up for a while.

As Sarah turned off the computer, she thought about the Steinberger's connection, since she worked for Steinberger's Department Store too. She shrugged it off as a coincidence. She was a secretary, not a sales associate. She placed the laptop back on the second-hand mahogany desk. Her new Stearns & Foster twin mattress looked more inviting than ever. The birds got less vocal. It was Saturday, and she didn't have to go to work. She crawled under the covers and drifted into dreamless sleep.

*

Saturday morning in southern Astoria, Queens: some early risers jogged, some headed toward Broadway for breakfast at a local diner or one of the many cafés, while others went to the supermarket farther down or the one up on 31st Avenue. Some went to the Korean and Mediterranean markets. A few lugged their laundry in shopping carts or plastic baskets to the launderettes in order to beat the 10 a.m. influx. Broadway and Steinway Streets were havens for affordable retail where supplies met the demand. There were the ubiquitous 99-cent stores. And if you couldn't get something at one Eckerd drugstore, there was another a few blocks away.

Sarah did none of the above. Life outside her apartment carried on without her knowledge or interference. She rolled over and hugged her pillow, wishing to stay low-key until ten.

Sarah slept longer than she had intended, and groaned because now her morning was starting later than planned. En route to the bathroom, she cursed.

Sarah haphazardly brushed her teeth, accidentally dropping her toothbrush into the sink. She yawned non-stop as toothpaste drooled from her mouth and onto her nightshirt. After rinsing her mouth, she splashed cold water on her face to revive herself. She wiped the mess off her nightshirt and finished her morning wash-up. She went to her closet and decided to put on plain white cotton underwear, a baggy brown T-shirt, faded jeans, and her dirty white sneakers. She combed her long messy strands and applied gloss to her dry lips. Her only piece of jewelry was a watch. Sarah, with her no-frills fashion sense and insecure demeanor, preferred to walk unnoticed.

Since money was tight, and she was somewhat of a loner, she had limited options for entertainment this weekend. She thought of checking out a movie at one of the theaters in Manhattan, but figured it was too late for a matinee. Still, Sarah longed to spend some quality time outside her neighborhood. She rushed out and bought a newspaper from the convenience store below. She opted for a quick meal at Dunkin' Donuts before boarding the elevated N train at Broadway.

Sarah's Manhattan odyssey was uneventful. The rerun of the 1999 movie *American Beauty* wasn't *Titanic* and Kevin

Spacey wasn't Leonardo DiCaprio. Sarah hated the reality of aging, or anything suburban. She'd had enough of the suburban lifestyle growing up on Long Island. The character Lester Burnham, played by Spacey, was in the throes of a mid-life crisis while dealing with his dysfunctional family. Sarah, a closet romantic, loved fantasy—she preferred watching a rich girl fall in love with a poor boy, only to lose him on a sinking ship in the icy Mid-Atlantic.

On the N train coming back to Astoria, her thoughts turned to Allie's story, and her nerves tightened like clock springs.

She stopped off for two slices of pepperoni pizza to go. She would open a bottle of Coke and watch TV while she ate. After that, she planned to take a shower, go to bed early, and forget about writing, but she reneged on her decision and wrote another chapter of the novel instead. Her keys moved with her thoughts.

"Fire, fire, Allie's head's on fire!"

Shrieks electrified the corridor of P.S. 10. Laughter formed a circle around the victim. Allie Harris's flustered tears couldn't wash away the filthy water poured from the janitor's corroded silver pail. She was the object of scorn again. Her pink cardigan offered no protection. Gray suds and grimy water seeped past the wool, violating her flesh, though her white go-go boots kept her feet dry.

Joey Coleman thought it would be fun getting even with that red-headed bitch, while winning his audience's attention.

11

He craved it more than candy. Allie was a loser. Her aunt and uncle had probably taken her out of the foster home for extra cash. From her fat head to her smelly toes, he hated everything about her. She was trash, a rodent, or perhaps a renegade roach from his dilapidated apartment. Worst of all, they were both loners. Joey worried about what the next decade would bring and the one after that. Multiplication at the blackboard scared him, but not as much as his future did. He, a skinny black boy, would have a much harder life than his plump, white opponent.

"Children, children! What's going on?" shouted Miss Thomas, a stout woman in her mid-fifties. "Stop this at once! Who was responsible for this? Tell me, or else all of you will be sent to detention and your parents will be notified immediately!"

Whispers buzzed amid the juvenile smirks and grins as Miss Thomas screeched her threats. Her bifocals slid down her beaked nose, allowing her eyes to instill fear into the minds of her pint-sized charges.

The pretty and petite Bonnie McGuire waved her hand, saying, "Miss Thomas, Miss Thomas, I know who did it!"

Order was restored after the culprit was exposed and the floor was mopped. Joey was reprimanded for his vicious prank. Allie was handed a towel to dry herself and a tissue to dry her tears.

Like Joey, Allie was no stranger to outbursts. Being different marked them as misfits, outsiders in a world of nasty kids with the genes of their equally nasty parents. They wore invisible tags that identified them on the game board of growing up.

Confidential information could spread like a five-alarm fire within the school community. Unfortunately, Bonnie's mother, Ann, the head of the PTA, was made privy to Allie's background through her friend, Margaret Lipson, the assistant principal, and told it to her best friend, Cheryl Katz, Sherry's mother.

During a craft class, Bonnie McGuire and her pretty brunette pal, Sherry Schulman, shared their mothers' gossip while applying clay to armatures, using Allie as their model. The exaggerated moldings suggested chubby flesh, topped with red strings for her hair. They knocked over their project, waiting for Allie's reaction. Bonnie blamed Allie for knocking it over. Both Bonnie and Sherry intended to place the head back on the armature, but first they wanted to pry it open to see if the 'Allie' head had brains.

Allie was no math whiz, but she could add up her adversaries' bullshit in seconds. She yelled, "Shut up, Bonnie, before I smack your lying head!"

Bonnie claimed that the reason Allie's hair was so red was that her mother had sex with the devil, just like in Rosemary's Baby.

"Rosemary's baby was a boy and his mother was raped, idiot! Why don't you read the book or go see the movie," retorted Allie.

Bonnie called Allie an imbecile and an evil child. She went on to opine that people hated her not only because she was stupid, fat, and ugly, but because she had been dumped in a foster home after her unwed mother died.

Miss Thomas shouted for the trio to behave. Without a judge or jury, the teacher overruled Allie's pleas, and passed her own verdict.

Miss Thomas escorted Allie to Principal Hughes's office. Principal Hughes called the Harris residence, and spoke with Gloria, Allie's aunt.

Gloria hurried to get dressed. In her haste, she ruined a pair of hose, but she had no time to find another. She grabbed her hat, coat, and gloves, and made a frenzied exit. As she walked toward Kingsbridge Avenue, the Bronx breeze stiffened her back and her fallen arches ached. She looked at her Timex. Her Irish temper, plus her impatience, made her want to strangle the minute hand.

She fidgeted on the corner as she waited for the light to change. She fixed her eyes on P.S. 10 across the street. As she tightened her lips, she was consumed by rage, her anger vaporizing into the bitter January air. "Wait until your uncle gets home tonight, my dear."

Sarah stopped typing. Her eyes began to hurt and she had to pee. After a trip to the bathroom, a second wave of energy hit her. She wrote:

Allie wished for her death and her uncle's as well. She knew that her wishes were sinful and that God would punish her,

14

but she had a right to feel this way, since God allowed bad things to happen. She wasn't her teacher's favorite, and she wasn't His favorite either. She was dumb and ugly, and could never compete with her cousin Mikey. Learning that she was illegitimate made the pain in her swollen cheek worse.

Even if she defended herself with the truth about what had happened at school, he would still hit her. Like a zombie, Aunt Gloria watched and said nothing. Uncle Abe was old and ugly, with slicked-back salt-and-pepper hair and a big hook nose. What did Aunt Gloria see in him? She was twelve years younger, blonde, and still pretty. They looked funny together. He had no money because he drank and gambled his Steinberger's paycheck away. On many occasions, Allie would catch him sticking his hands in the metallic treasure chest, stealing Cousin Mikey's and her money. "Uncle Sam should ship his ass to Vietnam," Allie thought.

Allie hid her head in the pillow. The damp pillowcase, a convenient handkerchief, did little to comfort her. The TV warfare of the show Combat! *from the living room replaced the earlier war that had taken place off-screen. Allie was too numb to hear it as her misery battled her brainwaves. An incessant buzz clogged her eardrums and kept her anguish concealed, never daring to leave her sanctum of privacy.*

She hated fairy tales. She especially hated the Disney characters on the dingy green wall. Like the blonde bimbo in her '50s blue gown, Cindy's escape was frozen in perpetual pursuit, her foot never reuniting with the missing glass slipper.

15

Why didn't they get her Mickey Mouse instead? Was it because her aunt had never found her Prince Charming? Her Spalding ball usually knocked Charming and Cindy off the wall. Eventually, their heads would fall off! Wouldn't Aunt Gloria love that?

Five years ago, the two-bedroom apartment had no space for a new addition to the Harris household. Aunt Gloria had almost lost Mikey in childbirth and was unable to have any more children. Her maternal need to have a daughter brought Allie into the fold.

It was cheaper to build a wall to divide the master bedroom into two, rather than to look for a larger place. The fabricated walls had 'ears' and heard everything. How many times would Uncle Abe complain about the hippie faggot crap on the radio? Allie had to keep the volume down; Motown music made his pressure boil.

Her aunt was on the telephone, complaining about all things related to the adult world, including the most recent incident at school. "Allie this and Allie that." It was always her fault that things went wrong. Not one word mentioned about Uncle Abe. As always, he got excused. Her crying intensified, and she wanted to drown in her pillow and die before dawn. Nevertheless, Allie kept the volume down. If she didn't, the door would open and Uncle Abe would leave another reminder of who was the boss.

By 2 a.m., her tears stopped. Shortly after, Allie fell asleep, still wearing her terrycloth slippers.

Sarah's keys moved faster, but not fast enough. She couldn't keep the dawn away from the window shade. She lived on the verge of a belated Y2K meltdown—her shame for not having a better job, her miserable boss, her fear of men, her lack of male companionship. Acknowledging that her brain cells needed recharging, she said, "Screw Allie. I'm going to bed."

Chapter 2

Sarah
(2001)

For the most part, Sarah's workweek went by uneventfully. Her nights had been dreamless, at least, and her subway commutes bearable. On Friday morning, Sarah arrived early to work, so as to give herself ample time to type the updated Fall Ready-to-Wear presentation memo for the copy director, Jill Myers, her 'darling' boss with the blonde highlights and perfect gym butt. Before Sarah was able to finish her muffin and coffee, the red light on her phone from Jill's extension lit up. Sarah stopped eating so she could listen to another one of her boss's high-pitched demands.

Jill barked, "Sar, did you finish the memo yet?"

"Give me a few minutes, please," said Sarah, already stressed out.

Sarah's boss ended the conversation with a *click*. Hidden behind flimsy cubbyhole walls, Sarah slammed the phone down, knowing that Jill would make her redo it five more times. Her boss's attitude toward her had changed over the past few months, becoming more distant and faultfinding. Sarah had lost a lot of sleep this past weekend. She had gone to the movies on Saturday, but the Queen Bitch wouldn't want to hear about it; Jill had stopped asking her about her weekends months ago. Perhaps

Sarah's activities weren't exciting enough? Sarah couldn't find a man to help cover her expenses and make her more sociably acceptable, nor could she afford to hang out, travel, learn to ski, play tennis, or go to fine restaurants. Sarah's salary barely covered the rent, food, and bills.

She gritted her teeth and slammed her fist on the keyboard. How she wished it were her lovely boss's face instead. She would love to pile-drive her and pin her Park Avenue ass to the floor, but Steinberger's HR would reward her with a long holiday at the Rikers Island Correctional Facility.

The phone rang again and Jill asked her to hurry up with the memo, reminding her that the presentation was at four. She insisted on calling Sarah "Sar."

Sarah held back her temper. She wanted to scream out, "*My name is Sarah, not Sar.*" She hated her boss for giving her a nickname that sounded like a disease. She almost clenched her teeth again, but stopped herself. Another trip to Dr. Horowitz would eat up her insurance and meager paycheck. She sat in her cubbyhole cell, defeated. She sipped on her three-hours-old coffee for instant inspiration. The boost of cold caffeine grounded her, and she returned to work, forgetting about sending that postcard from Rikers.

Shortly after, she got another phone call from her boss. Jill's persistence poked her nerves. Sarah lied and said she had only two lines to retype, although it was actually four. Jill's cell phone saved Sarah from another confrontation, giving her enough time to finish the memo for the meeting in twelve

19

minutes. She picked up the memo at the printer and handed it to Jill. The boss looked happier than usual, not because Sarah had finally *gotten it right,* but because her new boyfriend, Chip, was on the phone. Chip adored Jill's blonde hair, athletic body, and fancy job title as copy director. Like a Prada bag, she flaunted her success, prancing down the halls in her best Carrie Bradshaw pantomime, wearing Manolo Blahnik shoes, except she lacked Carrie's character.

With Sarah's biorhythms on the downslide, her lack of sleep greatly aggravated the general tedium of work. That dream-brat had become a chronic pest. Ever since Sarah moved out of the two-bedroom Bronx apartment on Kingsbridge Avenue to her red brick walk-up in Astoria, Queens, Allie had settled in as her nocturnal roommate.

Jill returned from the Fall Ready-to-Wear presentation victorious. The Queen smiled at Sarah, her earlier quibbles with her forgotten. Sarah felt relieved and grateful for Chip's chitchat. These moments almost brought her back to religion. Even better, Her Majesty was in a hurry to see her boyfriend. It was almost 6:30, and on Friday nights, single people got ready to swing into Saturday morning. Unfortunately, Sarah wasn't like most single gals in the Big Apple; at least not this Friday night. She could fake it next week if that brat would permit. Sarah's computer, like Sarah, ran on the slow side. She shut down her Mac, turned off the lamp, and removed her bag from the desk drawer. Before reaching the exit, she bumped into Jen Olsen, a copywriter for Men's Furnishings and Sarah's closest ally in the corporate barracks. Jen had also been her roommate for a month in the Kingsbridge Avenue apartment before moving to the Upper West Side.

"Hey, Sarah, let's head out to Second Avenue. There's a new hangout where we can pick up some hunks tonight. You know, you should try to get out once in a while. Don't let the Wicked Bitch of the East Side screw up your ovaries for life."

At the elevator, Sarah turned to her friend apologetically and said, "Look, Jen, I really can't. I'm PMSing and had a sleepless night. I'm not in the best condition to cruise the bars tonight. Maybe next week?"

"I understand. *No problema, Señorita Kahn.* Take it easy this weekend, girlfriend. Get some rest. You'll need it as long as you still work for her."

The employees' elevator finally arrived. Sarah and Jen crowded into the subway-like box. Their conversation paused, each floor, a countdown to freedom, although they knew the vicious cycle would be waiting for them at the employees' entrance on Monday morning.

Sarah said, "Goodbye, Jen. Have a great weekend."

Jen answered, "Ditto. Please take care of yourself. You're looking too thin these past few weeks. Take it easy, okay?"

They waved goodbye. The fashionably svelte Jen rushed uptown to Wellington's and a possible date, while plain Sarah slowly headed to Rockefeller Center to catch the Astoria-bound N train, after which she would walk three blocks east from the elevated Broadway station to her one-bedroom apartment, where she would sleep alone tonight.

*

Sarah followed the crowd down the iron steps of the El to the street. The light, in her favor, enabled her to dash across to the northern side of Broadway. She walked the three blocks to her building, bypassing the laughter and music that streamed from the outdoor cafés. She reached her apartment door and it took three tries for her to unlock it. Once inside, a pregnant roach greeted her, and Sarah's Nine West pumps crushed the mother-to-be to death. After cleaning the mess off her floor and heels, she put a frozen dinner in the microwave. She poured a glass of Gallo Chardonnay and turned on *Wheel of Fortune*. She preferred drowning her misery with wine as she reassured herself that the $800 rental wasn't a pricey mistake. It wasn't worth sharing that renovated apartment near Riverdale in the Bronx with Kate Robbins, and Dana Chu, paying a third of the rent and the Con Ed bill. Privacy came at a high price, and her $28,000-a-year pittance as a glorified servant to Ms. Myers restricted her escape from Queens.

She pressed the remote button and jogged from channel to channel, and her mind did likewise. As the wine lured her deeper into dejection, Sarah couldn't concentrate on any show. She reflected on her recent history; how she had pinched bucks to take night courses in Communications at NYU last year, while selling, filing, and typing. She had lucked out getting copywriting temp jobs at two established ad agencies and a slick

22

up-and-coming fashion magazine. It wasn't easy for a working-class girl from Franklin Square, Long Island, to succeed when all parental concern had gone toward the education of her two brothers, Joe and Sam. Being an unplanned addition to the Kahn household, her birth had added financial stress on her dad. His small appliance shop in Franklin Square didn't provide enough income to support a family of five. Her dad would sometimes take out his frustrations on the boys, either with the back of his hand or the strap, but with Sarah, it was much more frequent.

Back in the '80s, Oakwood Central High School was good enough for an average-looking girl from Maple Street being groomed for marriage. Even the name of the street was nondescript. She graduated with mediocre grades, but she would have done better if she had been encouraged. It came eight years later, when Serena McCoy, a new copywriter at Focus NYC, advised Sarah to go back to school if she wanted a one-way ticket out of the typing pool. Back then, it was about *getting the ring*. A decent office job in the City would attract marriageable prospects, not Tom Barchek and his halitosis. She had to get out of suburbia and the cookie-cutter lifestyle being planned for her. Mr. Right would have a large bank account and a Beemer, and live in a fabulous tower guarded by a doorman who would whistle for a cab to Bloomingdale's Department Store, just like in *Splash*.

Her empty wine glass represented her love life. Forget about marriage and motherhood, and her ovaries might as well be scrambled eggs. She would get fat and have hot flashes like

23

her mother. She poured more wine, meandering further into a funk.

She had retired Mr. Right, who probably lived in a Dorian Gray-like '80s music video. She was getting older and was learning to be more self-sufficient. She could write an ad in seconds, except her darling boss wouldn't approve her promotion. She got more entangled in Jill's web, and each memo turned into a noose. She had done some freelance work for Focus NYC magazine and at Wayne Brandt Advertising Agency and Victor Thomas Associates, Inc. before getting a full-time position as Ms. Jill's personal slave. At Focus NYC, Sarah's talent had impressed Jackie Friedman, and Jackie told her to keep in touch in case an opening became available. The years passed, and the recommendation probably got filed under "Oblivion." She called several times, but the *secretary du jour* would give her the routine; *send another résumé and cover letter for the active file*. "Active file," of course, was a euphemism for dumping your résumé and cover letter into the wastepaper basket and into the recycle dump, a form of reincarnation for junked letters to come back as new résumés and cover letters, taking the job market roller coaster again, and having more lives than a cat.

Andy Zarelli, the copy director at Focus, had left for the West Coast a year ago. He respected her for taking Communications courses at NYU. He saw potential behind the mousy-brown hair. He promised to hire her if there was an opening. But when she called him six months later, his roommate, Otis, told her that he had died from AIDS. She

24

lamented that she hadn't called him sooner, not for her own selfish needs, but as a friend.

Too much wine messed with her head. She sped up the nightly washing of dishes, lingerie, and herself. After putting the toothpaste back in the medicine cabinet, Sarah stared at the mirror, wondering if she would be okay tonight—reddened eyes never lied. In her haste to expedite her bathroom ritual, she nearly knocked over the toiletries on the sink. Being too tired, she forgot to flush. Only the bed and the darkness knew whether that child would be back again. She stumbled toward the bedroom, flicked the light switch off, and collapsed into bed. Except for the digital tick-tocks, all sounds faded into the blackness.

Sarah had another dream. This time it took place in a kitchen with dated appliances from her parents' generation. She looked at the clock on the nightstand. In six hours, the alarm would be buzzing.

Her restlessness paced with the clock. For the next hour she tossed in bed, before pounding out her frustrations on the keyboard. As she began to type, it dawned on her that there was another Steinberger's connection.

"Allie, will you get up already? Time to go to school," yelled Gloria from the kitchen.

Gloria began talking to herself. "Damn kid, always a problem, just like her mother. Siobhan, why did you do this to me? Why am I such a nebbish for trouble? I married a lazy Jewish schmuck who can't earn a living. He never even completed high school. According to Abe's family, I'm his dumb shiksa wife from the Irish Bronx. They keep praising him like he's God's gift to me. He's just a damn clerk! He doesn't bring home the bacon, but he sure does eat it. What a goy I am! I should have married Joey Malone, the mechanic—at least he's doing well with his air-conditioning and refrigeration business in Flatbush, Brooklyn." She lowered her voice so that no one in the house could overhear her.

Allie heard Aunt Gloria's command, but she could barely get out of bed. The pillow provided minimal comfort for her swollen face. A few minutes passed before Allie came into the kitchen and said good morning to her aunt.

Seeing Abe's handiwork across her niece's left cheek made Gloria nervous, and she worried about what Miss Thomas, or the classmates, might suspect about the Harris household. Her unsteady hands dropped the box of Corn Flakes, scattering its contents across the linoleum floor.

Allie took her seat by the Formica kitchen table and tried to camouflage her tears in the Corn Flakes. She was not cut out to be a soldier in the urban trenches. The kitchen, traditionally a haven for women to find temporary shelter away from men, was no longer safe, especially with her uncle's job-related problems mounting.

She heard a barrage of cigarette-induced coughs coming toward the kitchen. Allie didn't want to face the enforcer this morning, but how could she avoid him? She searched for solace

26

staring at the faux green-marbled linoleum. Fear made her face hurt more.

Gloria worked frantically to clean up the Corn Flakes. Puffing a Lucky Strike, her overweight spouse stood like a human chimney in the doorway between the kitchen and the foyer. He grimaced as he watched his kneeling wife clean up the cereal. His uncombed hair gave him the look of a wild beast, and his belly shook behind his wife-beater shirt as inflammatory words about his financial losses bellowed from his mouth.

"Gloria, what the hell did you do? Wanna make the Kellogg family richer this weekend? Wanna buy another box of cereal instead of saving for Mikey's college tuition? That kid is a senior at Bronx Science and he's college material for NYU. Do you want him to be like me, a working stiff for Steinberger's Accounts Payable? I lost out on a raise this year, and now I'll never be anything more than a clerk. His Nibs, Mr. Moran, blames my absenteeism on my kidneys. The guys in the office tell me that the big shots prefer younger blood with college degrees."

Gloria said, "Sorry, Abe, I was in a hurry. I'm concerned about Allie's face."

"Why are you tied up in knots about her? Come on, Gloria, she's a mistake born from a bigger one," snarled Abe.

"Abe, don't talk about Siobhan like that! Let her rest in peace, for Christ's sake! She made a bad decision, and I'm sorry I didn't help her when she needed me. If I had, she would be alive today."

27

Abe yelled, "Yeah, and we wouldn't have her kid eating us out of house and home. What a waste! If you wanted a stray, why didn't you take in an alley cat? Would have been a helluva lot cheaper and less trouble!"

His hazel eyes, like knives, faced Allie's, ready to inflict more pain. "Why are you getting so bent out of shape, Missy? You can't get through a school year without a trip to the principal's office?"

"It's not her fault that the schwartze kid threw dirty water on her," protested Gloria.

"Hey, what about our own kind!" shouted Abe. "She can't even get along with the white kids. She should learn to grow up and stop being a fuckin' whiner."

His eyes darted back to his niece, yelling, "Hey, Allie, stick to the books like Mikey instead of picking fights and acting so fuckin' stupid!"

"I'm not fuckin' stupid, damn it," screamed Allie. She needed to vent, and whether she did or not, her uncle would hit her.

"Are you daring me again, Missy? Would you like me to wash your filthy mouth with soap? Like your right cheek to match the other one?" Abe's face turned the color of Hell and his right hand clenched into a fist.

"Abe, stop it! She's just a child. She has to go to school, and you must get to work on time. Please, not now! Abe, you're red as a beet, your pressure, please, not now. Look at her face! What will the school say this time?"

28

Abe's face paled at the sight of his son in the doorway. His fist relaxed, as he greeted Mikey, his future CEO.

Mikey asked about the commotion in the kitchen, but his dad said 'nothin', nothin' at all.' With a semi-yawn, Mikey headed for his chair by the dinette and poured the milk into his cereal. He read the terror on his mother's face, and especially in his cousin's almond-brown eyes. Her uncle had left his mark on her cheek. It was her turn to take the brunt of life. Mom had had hers when she first married him, until she got lucky after being sent to the hospital with a broken nose. After that incident, he never touched her again. It was his turn to step into the ring. He had learned to duck by being passive. He had learned to hide behind his books and dreams. His dad respected him for being studious. If only Allie would be less stubborn. He had tried to teach her the art of survival, but Dad needed to take out his frustrations on someone, and poor Allie was his whipping girl. She wasn't his flesh and blood, and she would never be part of the family. How could she ever be accepted at school when people knew that she was illegitimate? Mom had told him that she was sorry she had confided in Joan Conrad. They had been the best of friends and bridge buddies, and Mom had spilled her heart to her over wine. The alcohol must have gone to Joan's lips during that Saturday night get-together at Margaret Lipson's. Mom overheard Joan's conversation with Margaret in the kitchen. Out of embarrassment, she left early. That was the last time she played cards and socialized with the women of Kingsbridge Women's Club. Joan lit the match, and from ear to

29

ear, the gossip spread. No wonder the kids at school resented his cousin. They were only mimicking their parents. "Allie, you just can't win," thought Mikey.

As for his mother, she had come from a lower middle-income home, and divorce wasn't an option. Dad donated a good portion of his Steinberger's paycheck to the bookie and the bartenders at the Court Pub near the store. An office job or sales position wouldn't provide security for a single woman with two children. She only had a high school degree and was trained to serve those above her station. "Mom, you can't win either."

Dressed in his worn-out Goodman & Suss pinstripe suit, with his hair slicked back, Abe returned to the kitchen to gulp down his lukewarm coffee. Traces of brown dripped down his chin, and he wiped it with a tissue before running off to work. Gloria finished her first hour and a half of housewife duty, handing the lunch bags to the children and sending them off to school.

Before Allie could finish buttoning her jacket, her aunt whispered in her ear, "Don't say anything about last night or this morning. If anyone asks about the bruise, just say that you slammed your cheek against the edge of the door when you fell off the kitchen chair."

She kissed her on the head and nodded to Mikey. He led the fourth-grader down the stairwell and said, "Try to cheer up, and stay away from the old man. Just let the big jerk blow his stack until his steam gives out."

Allie faked a smile, observing the black-and-white marbled squares in the lobby. Once outside, she waved goodbye to him. The sun almost blinded her. However, she didn't mind it. Mr. Sunshine painted a storybook picture, using her block as a backdrop. Even the garbage cans looked beautiful. She breathed in the autumn air and it soothed her aching cheek. It was one of these rare moments that made her feel free, and it felt good to be alone.

Chapter 3

Sarah
(2001)

Sarah's Monday morning marathon to get to work on time came with extra challenges—a run in the left heel of her DKNY pantyhose and her bra cutting into her skin. Missing the N train convinced her that bad luck really did come in threes. As the train disappeared along the erector set-like route into Long Island City, Sarah wished that Jill would do the same. Sarah blamed her ill fortune on her alarm clock, Allie's dream-write, and herself for wanting to write a novel. The wind brushed Sarah's left cheek, leaving a lingering pain. She thought that she saw Allie hiding behind arms and torsos on the crowded platform. Her imagination was obviously working overtime.

Twelve minutes later, another train arrived at Broadway. The child stepped back, allowing Sarah and the other passengers to board. Sarah turned around, but Allie disappeared.

At 9:45 a.m., Sarah arrived at her Steinberger's cubbyhole. Thankfully, Jill was busy arguing about the maintenance contract for her Park Avenue condo. Sarah scooted to her chair, unnoticed, like that child who hadn't boarded the train.

After another mundane day at work, Sarah made her routine trip to the ladies' room before her routine commute home to, hopefully, a night of solitude and sleep without Allie invading her dreams. When the N train pulled into the Broadway station, Sarah followed the crowd down the elevated stairs. She headed for the Korean grocery store to buy utilitarian necessities to fill her empty stomach, if not her empty life—a quart of 99 percent fat-free skim milk, a half dozen eggs to add back the fat taken out of the milk, and a loaf of whole wheat bread to satisfy the communion given only to herself. Funny that she should think about religion, when she was an absentee Christian with a Jewish surname. Her father was Jewish, her mom was Episcopalian, and Sarah was agnostic. She threw in a head of Romaine lettuce, some unblemished vine tomatoes, and yogurt salad dressing. As a single girl, she felt she had to watch her weight.

She walked alone, invisible amid the activity along Broadway on the cusp of a warm May evening. Laughing couples passed by, holding hands. Smiling faces smoked cigarettes and sipped cappuccinos outside Greek cafés. A gentle breeze accommodated their beautiful mood. Sarah wondered if she should try the dating scene again. Her ex-boyfriends probably thought that she was ready to checkmate them into marriage. Her private areas were private, and there was no trespassing without her consent. Wet kisses should attract saliva freaks and French kisses belonged in a snake pit. She had heard from many women that free meals were usually paid off in bed. Some women told her not to feel sorry for herself, while others claimed that they felt sorry for her. Sometimes the nicest ones were bitches in disguise. Jen happened to be a sweetheart, but could Sarah trust her?

Her tampon would screw her tonight—*thank God for safe sex.*

Sarah's period came on schedule, making her sleepier than usual, with mega cramps. However, the ibuprofen wasn't kicking in. She plugged in the heating pad, allowing ten minutes to pass for the heat to help her get six hours of nirvana.

*

Like Chanticleer, the clock sounded off at seven. Sarah cursed and rolled over, hoping that an extra forty-five minutes would alleviate the cramps. Sarah couldn't mess with either Mother Nature's or life's schedule. Her punishment would be lateness and additional stress getting to work.

Her pace quickened after gulping down some orange juice. Her corporate and sexual greasepaint would have to wait until she got to the office and her tummy would have to endure a partial fast until she could order tea and oatmeal from Java Muffin. In an attempt to look professional, she put on her black A-line dress and a strand of pearls. She crammed her feet into her Nike sneakers and threw her two-inch black pumps into a tote bag before dashing out, defying pain and sluggish legs.

The N train pulled in at exactly 8:10. She boarded the packed train, hoping that by Queensboro Plaza, one comfortable passenger would vacate a seat. For two days in a row, someone else had been beating Sarah to that precious dollar-fifty seat. The twenty-something able-bodied man pushed in front of her and got first choice for the coveted last seat. He sat immersed in the *Daily News*, oblivious to Sarah's scowl and discomfort.

34

A female passenger noticed Sarah and asked, "Are you all right?" She offered Sarah her seat, and she accepted, thanking the woman for her kindness. Once in the seat, Sarah hugged her tote and bag against her stomach.

From the loudspeaker boomed the mechanical announcement: "Lexington Avenue, 59th Street, next stop. Stand clear of the closing doors, please!" The doors closed and the train continued on its route toward the brick-and-mortar tunnel, as Sarah entered her dream-world:

The sky, neither day nor night, became a bleak gray-blue backdrop to frame a leafless tree. Red flames sprouted from the tree's skeletal branches, and blood replaced its sap and dripped like tears. The tree bled, as an eerie sound reverberated within its bark, down to its roots and into the parched soil. The fire looked fierce, yet it didn't consume the bark. Wounded and dying, the tree moaned as the wind slapped the flames. The tree lifted its branches, before . . .

Sarah woke up on the floor of the subway car. Some passengers inquired whether she was okay and a woman yelled for someone to pick her up. One man claimed that she wasn't breathing right, while another prayed for her. Among the few grumblers, one said that she was just looking for an excuse not to go to work, and another complained about being late again. A woman cried out for medical assistance and a man told the conductor to call 9-1-1.

The train halted but started up again before terminating at Lexington Avenue in Manhattan. An announcement about a

35

sick passenger caused more confusion and griping as the straphangers filed out.

The woman who had given her the seat handed Sarah a bottle of water. "Honey, take a sip of water. You looked like you were having a nightmare. You were moaning and gasping for breath when the train pulled out of Queensboro Plaza. Now inhale slowly and take a few more sips. Atta girl! You're getting your color back. Keep breathing in and out. Don't worry, help is on the way."

"You're the one who gave me the seat," said Sarah drowsily. "I did have a scary dream. I'm also feeling lousy because of my period."

"Just drink and rest. By the way, did you have any breakfast?"

Sarah confessed that she'd only had orange juice. The woman shook her head and handed her a granola bar. Sarah thanked her and began nibbling on it. From the corner of her left eye, she thought she saw Allie appear and disappear, like yesterday on the Broadway platform. A sudden chill made her shoulders tremble.

The police arrived ten minutes later, armed with notebooks and questions, and the medics came two minutes after. Sarah refused medical attention, since the water and food had helped her regain her strength. She apologized again for any inconvenience before being escorted out of the train with the Good Samaritan, whose name was Sara Weinstein. As it turned

36

out, this Sara also worked for Steinberger's, as the new buyer for the Housewares Division.

The raven-haired Sara advised Sarah to get a late pass before going to work, but the clerk in the nearest booth had an attitude, so the buyer insisted on seeing the stationmaster, who wrote the pass.

Ms. Weinstein advised, "You should contact your boss. The pass will back you up for lateness. Who is your boss, anyway?"

Sarah answered, "Jill Myers. But I don't own a cell phone."

"You work for Ms. Jill Hot to Trot? I'll call her as soon as we get out of the subway. What a character, pretending that it wasn't her fault that my Cuisinart ad ran wrong in the Sunday *Times*. I presented the correct copy to her at the monthly newsprint meeting. However, the copy chief and his writer weren't present. After calling her and Production on the status of my ad, the proof finally showed up two days prior to release with a dummy copy. I did get calls from Production and Copy claiming that they had no actual copy to work with. Did Ms. Jill ever return my calls or emails? No! I had to bring a duplicate fact sheet to the Copy Division and get my proof re-circulated later that afternoon. And I had to adjust the error made on the price; the ditz typed it backwards. I asked Production for the revised proof by five, and this time the price was correct. But the document with the wrong price was transmitted to *The Times*. Your boss Jill was responsible for this fiasco."

Sara hailed a cab outside Levi's. While stuck in traffic, the buyer called and left a message on Jill Myers's answering machine. They arrived at their destination at 9:24 a.m. and stopped by Java Muffin. Sarah reneged on the tea and oatmeal, and they both left with coffee and muffins.

Based on the story, Sarah knew that this person was also Jill Myers's nemesis, and her fears intensified as Sara escorted her to Jill's office.

Jill saw the Housewares buyer outside her door with her hapless, muffin-chewing secretary. The buyer said hi to Jill and gave a brief explanation for Sarah's tardiness. After the buyer said goodbye, Sarah went to her cubicle without her buffer to help her out for the rest of the day.

The Nokia theme from inside Jill's Louis Vuitton tote derailed her annoyance with Sarah. Another call from Jill's boyfriend sweetened her mood, and she promised Chip that she would see him for drinks tonight. She dialed her secretary and said, "Sar, when you settle down, please see me!"

Sarah sensed trouble and spit her corn muffin into the napkin. Zombie-like, she obeyed her boss's command. Once in the office, she waited for Jill to make the first move.

Jill motioned for Sarah to take a seat and said, "Sarah, are you having problems working here? Are you having some personal issues?"

Sarah didn't want to answer Jill's question. Caught behind closed doors, she observed her boss's manicured claws and wondered what else could go wrong today.

"The reason I called you in is that I'm concerned about your health. You've been looking haggard since you moved to your new apartment in Queens. I don't mean to pry, but I've noticed a change in you over the past week. You fainted in front of another employee, who will probably spread gossip about a member of my team. Remember last week when she had a hissy fit over how we run this department, even though it was she who was irresponsible? If she was so concerned about her ad, why didn't she call two weeks earlier? You know how the copy people constantly screw up with their information sheets."

Jill thought that perhaps she shouldn't be too hard on Sarah. "By the way, if you need to take a day off to recuperate, why not take tomorrow, which happens to be Friday. I'm sure you could use a three-day weekend. Better yet, how about working half a day today and starting your three-day weekend sooner. You can leave after eating lunch. Does two o'clock sound reasonable?"

Baffled by her boss's sudden benevolence, Sarah expressed her gratitude and apologized for sounding abrasive.

After Sarah left and closed the door behind her, Jill fidgeted with her Mark Cross pen, while her other perfectly rounded Essie hand tapped on the desk. She stared out the window, as the sun cast shadows on the western side of the street. The phone rang—it was her private number; however, Jill decided not to answer it. Her mind focused instead on what to do about Sarah. She needed someone more efficient, proactive, and outgoing to take her place. She unlocked the cabinet by her desk

39

and removed a manila folder stuffed with résumés of candidates who had been recommended by colleagues and friends. She pondered before placing the folder into her tote.

Jill dialed Sarah to tell her that she would be leaving for a luncheon at 12:30 and to expect her to return around two. Jill also reminded Sarah to leave as soon as she returned.

"No problem, Jill. Do you wish to take this call from Tom Hong, the sales rep from Focus NYC magazine?"

Jill almost forgot about Tom Hong and the contract, and took the call.

Sarah transferred the call, wishing that her days with Jill would be over soon. Tom had reassured her that there was still an opening in Copy at Focus NYC. He was aware that Jackie Friedman had been impressed with her when she did freelance work for the company. He promised Sarah that he would remind Jackie. Sarah hoped that he would know better than to divulge this to Jill.

Jill touched up her makeup; Clinique lip gloss to lubricate her mouth, some Bobbi Brown to accentuate her high cheekbones, and MAC to highlight her large hazel eyes. She brushed her blonde shoulder-length locks and spritzed some Vera Wang. She approved of what she saw in the mirror. She zipped up her makeup pouch, locked her closet, and scooted out the door. She passed by Sarah's desk, letting her *goodbye* disappear with her scent. Her secretary shook her head, thinking, *Yeah, good riddance. I hope you choke on your artichoke.*

40

Sarah dialed Jen and asked, "Wanna break for lunch? The Queen Bitch just left the premises and won't be back until two. She told me to pack my ass out of here when she returns. The receptionist will take her calls. She even gave me tomorrow off. How sweet is that? It has something to do with what went down this morning. I'll fill you in on the details over Caesar salad and pink lemonade."

They both said 'okay' and 'ad infinitum' as they walked together to the ladies' room.

*

Sarah and Jen went to Java Muffin for lunch. After paying for their meals, they carried their trays to a remote table. It was 1:00 and crowded, so they were relegated to the unfortunate two-seater next to the garbage bin. Jen got the knives and forks. Sarah pried open the pre-measured salad dressing cup and poured it over her Romaine lettuce, sorry she had not asked for another cup. She savored the pink lemonade—feeling stronger with each sip.

Sarah recounted the bizarre events. "It all started when I had these weird dreams about a girl called Allie and, this morning, a bleeding tree on fire. Well, I'm using this material for a novel I'm writing."

*

Jill sat down for lunch with her friend at La Rue de Belle Fleur. She liked this quiet upscale restaurant on Madison Avenue. She hated the world of plebeian salads and plastic flatware, cups, bowls, and trays carried to plastic chairs, and pseudo-wooden tables occupied by loud-mouthed office workers and lower-level executives.

Jill unfolded her rose linen napkin and requested San Pellegrino water. She preferred keeping her senses intact during luncheons—alcohol was best consumed after hours when she was with Chip. Her guest requested Merlot.

The waiter returned with the water and wine, and asked if they wanted to order. The woman across from her said *oui,* and read the orders in French to impress the haughty young *garçon.* He approved the selections: steamed oysters in white wine sauce over Moroccan-style couscous, and venison braised in burgundy and cranberry sauce, served with Yukon potatoes and broccoli. He said *merci beaucoup* and disappeared behind closed doors to chew out the busboy for not serving the bread basket to his customers, while the apprentice cooks struggled to keep up with the demands of the lunchtime crowd, and especially those from the impatient head chef.

A short time later, the busboy brought a basket filled with assorted grain rolls and bread slivers, accompanied by butter rosettes and ceramic cups of jams and preserves, and placed it regally before the ladies in waiting.

Jill selected a whole wheat roll and broke it in half, spreading a little butter on one side and some raspberry preserves on top of it. She looked away from the roll and said, "I need your advice on something, or maybe I should say, about someone."

"Sure, Jill. Tell me, and I'll see what I can do for you."

Before two o'clock, Sarah and Jen returned to the tenth floor of Steinberger's. This floor, the eleventh, and the twelfth floors were the employee sections and, thus, off limits to the customers. All marketing, public relations, and advertising were on the tenth floor. The merchants controlled the eleventh floor, and the CEO and his entourage of directors and vice presidents executed business from the twelfth. The pressure to move merchandise and to outdo the competition went on as usual here.

The two associates were no strangers to pressure; they breathed it in daily—Jen felt it when she wrote copy, and Sarah, when she coordinated Jill's meetings. They tried to squeeze into an unwritten requirement—*dress well and kiss ass.* Both women needed to keep their jobs, recalling what had happened to one of the sales associates last week when a Sutton Place matron, while holding her yappy Pomeranian, verbally abused the poor girl for not finding another Nicole Miller dress in a size six.

By 2:15, Jill's lack of time management was getting on Sarah's nerves. After two hours, not even a phone from Jill about the delay.

From Jill's window, Sarah watched clouds pace toward Manhattan, looking like pretty marshmallows against the azure sky. Like Allie, she knew that pretty things sometimes lacked pretty intentions. The bloated clouds darkened as her cramps returned.

At 4:52, Jill stormed into the office, holding several shopping bags from Henri Bendel, which she plopped outside Sarah's cubicle.

Her words hit like a thunderbolt. "Why didn't you leave after lunch?"

"Jill, you told me to wait until you returned. You never got around to giving me your cell number in case I had to reach you. You never told me where you were having lunch, nor did you tell me that you were going shopping. I had no choice but to stay here. Besides, Angela Somaso from Better Sweaters called again about the Christmas campaign, and I have a couple of messages from this rep who wants to plug her new magazines. She faxed me the media kit and will FedEx the hard copy for tomorrow's delivery."

Sarah held the fax in her hand, but her boss preferred to look at the large raindrops that were beating against the window.

She said, "Sar, you may leave now. I hope you feel better. Have a restful weekend and thanks for minding the fort. Sorry about the rain."

Sarah couldn't fight Mother Nature's will, Jill's selfishness, or her own bad luck. She answered, "Don't worry, Jill. I have an umbrella in my drawer. Thanks again, and have a great weekend."

Chapter 4

Sarah
(2001)

Although Sarah had an unusually swift commute home, getting caught in a thunderstorm, as well as Jill's disrespectful and cavalier treatment, ruined her day. The three flights to her one-bedroom flat became three times the challenge, with the stress from the past week adding weight to each ankle. In her left hand, she held a Chase Visa bill and an envelope addressed from Focus NYC.

Her clammy fingers fumbled with the double lock and she dropped her shoulder-strap bag, plastic tote, and mail in the process. After several attempts, the correct keys slipped in. She kicked the door against the doorstop and slammed it before locking herself in for the night.

The red light on the answering machine flashed, prompting her to listen to her messages: one from her mother, asking her to be considerate and call her more often, and the other from Jen, who wanted to know if Sarah had gotten home okay. She would deal with the calls later.

She ripped open the envelope from Focus NYC. The last two sentences read:

Your referral letters from Wayne Brandt Advertising Agency and Victor Thomas Associates, Inc. solidify you as a potential

candidate for our expanding copy team at Focus NYC. Please
call to make an appointment for an interview, and bring a
portfolio of your most recent work.

The thought of being interviewed by Jackie Friedman relieved some of her distress, and even her damp clothes felt less damp. Her optimistic mood gave her the incentive to dial her mom. Her family would be surprised, since she rarely had any good news to share, but when no one answered the phone, she left a brief message. Then she called Jen.

Usually, Sarah felt at ease with Jen, but tonight her friend's *congratulations* seemed a tad lukewarm. A few seconds later, Sarah heard a knock, which Jen heard from her end too.

Jen asked, "What's that all about, Sarah? Is the landlord complaining about another leak in your apartment?"

"I'll check to see who's at the door," she said.

She put the receiver down on the IKEA table and slid the peephole cover to the side. No one was there. As soon as she turned away, there was another knock, except this time louder and more relentless, sending chills up and down her back. Sarah panicked again when she slid the peephole cover and saw no one. She opened the door as far as the security lock's chain would permit, and shouted, "Who is it?" Chills crept up her spine again as she checked the empty hall. From the receiver, Jen's voice cried out, "Sarah, are you all right? Should I call the cops? Sarah, please answer me! Sarah!"

Sarah unlocked the chain and ran down the stairwell. All the doors were closed and no one was lurking behind the stairs.

46

Sarah shivered in the hallway and hurried back to her apartment, closing the door and locking both the top and bottom locks. She heard Jen's shrieks and grabbed the phone. "No one's around. Maybe it came from a neighbor. You know this apartment isn't soundproof, with these cardboard walls and plywood doors. I think I'll call it a night and try to get some rest. It's been a very long week. Good night, Jen, and thanks for looking after me."

Jen said, *"No problema.* Oh, by the way, the reason I called tonight was to tell you that I'm leaving Steinberger's in two weeks. I got a great sales position at *The New Yorker*. More money and status."

"Jen, you never told me that you were looking for another job," snapped Sarah.

"Sarah, I was going to tell you over lunch, but you weren't in any condition to listen."

Sarah yawned, asked if they could talk tomorrow, and hung up without saying good night. She found it strange that Jen had suddenly become less open, and that communication with Kate Robbins and Dana Chu had dramatically lessened after she moved to Astoria. Out of revenge, Sarah started deleting Kate's and Dana's calls and emails.

Goosebumps fondled her arms as she turned counterclockwise away from the phone. For a humid evening, her entire apartment felt oddly cool. The A/C was off and the windows were closed.

She headed for the bathroom and undressed for a quick shower, turning on the hot water valve for extra steam. She suddenly felt as if she was coming down with a virus. After the shower, she dressed in her nightshirt, panties, and robe. She had a cup of chicken soup before retiring to the bedroom for a night of much-needed sleep.

She placed the letter on her desk and flicked the light switch off on the nightstand lamp. She crawled under the comforter, seeking warmth, but the chills moved from her back, downward, to caress her slim thighs. She fell asleep, but the chill traveled underneath her nightshirt and up her spine again, until it crossed over her shoulders and down to her breasts.

She didn't know whether to resist or not as the sensation tickled her nipples in a circular motion. Her nipples hardened as the invisible hands continued to massage each breast. Her animal instinct desired more, and she permitted the hands to fondle her breasts more savagely—cold lips tenderly kissed her nipples—its warm tongue washed and soothed them. She couldn't move or scream but didn't wish for this to end. She surrendered to whatever the lips, tongue, and fingers wanted to do.

She woke up breathless, soaked in perspiration. Her body reeked with a peculiar odor mixed with her own natural scent. She reminded herself that it was only a dream. Her heartbeat resumed to a normal rhythm, and she assured herself that the heavy sweating was caused by some hormonal and viral concoction. She removed and discarded the messy tampon and inserted a fresh one. She washed the bloodstains from her panties and shirt. However, the shirt's buttons had been ripped off, just

48

like in the dream. Her erotic escapade left her a little shaky, and she dropped the soap on the tiled floor.

In the floor-length mirror behind the bathroom door, her breasts looked swollen, with scratches etched in blood. She felt odd touching them while washing herself in the tub. The feeling of pleasure mixed with pain confused her. Like a phantom tongue, the warm washcloth gently soothed her nipples. She watched them harden lustfully, enjoying each caress of the washcloth. She ached to relive the sensation, but something felt off-kilter.

After the shower, she nervously threw on a clean T-shirt and panties. She went to the living room and saw the flashing red light on her answering machine. According to the machine, Jen had left two messages: one at 8:20 and the other at 9:46. It was 11:10, and Sarah thought she might still be up. Her fingers kept hitting the wrong numbers until the third try.

Jen answered, but Sarah's words sounded garbled, and her friend asked her to repeat what she had said. Between sobs, Sarah managed to convey the details of her weird dream.

*

Twenty minutes later, the phone call ended. Speaking to Jen did little to console her. Her friend's soliloquy on how fear could run amok in dreams hardly calmed her. Dream or no dream, she was unsettled by what had happened to her. *Was it self-inflicted?* Yet she couldn't forget the excitement—her passion became an obsession. Jen's analysis was that Sarah needed to "chill out and be more open to love."

49

Although thunder rattled the windows, Sarah swam in her own storm. But raindrops had that hypnotic effect of relieving tension, and today was her day off. She went to the kitchen for a glass of skim milk and a chocolate chip cookie— her pre-breakfast. At almost half past five, it was still dark out. After eating, her sloppy bed looked more desirable than ever. She wrapped herself in the cocoon of the blanket and fell asleep.

*

In her dream, darkness surrounded her, and she yearned for another sexual encounter. But instead, she saw ten-year-old Allie sitting on her divan, forcing herself to do her Social Studies assignment. She had a black eye. Once again, Sarah became both the spectator and outsider in the evolving saga of Allie Harris—and once again, she would have to be the ghostwriter upon her waking hour.

She saw Allie, but Allie didn't see her. The child shifted restlessly, testing different positions for comfort. But she got nowhere with her studies. She had a bruised cheek and started to cry, disturbing her uncle in the living room.

Her uncle banged on the door, and Allie said, "I'm studying for my Social Studies test. Miss Thomas says that . . ."

With brute force, Uncle Abe swung the door open, damaging both the doorknob and the wall. Had they been human, blood would have stained them. The dent on the doorknob's metal frame would have resulted in a concussion. The chipped wall would have required immediate surgery. It was

50

impossible for Sarah to intervene in a forty-year time span that was stuck in a dream. All she could do was watch.

The uncle called her a stupid baby for not producing better grades. She pleaded with him to stop insulting her and promised that she would try to study harder. After her uncle smacked her head and face again, she sobbed like a beggar.

Although he had lost his job due to his chronic kidney problems, he accused Allie for ruining his health and career, and she cried, "I'm sorry, Uncle Abe, please forgive me! I didn't mean for you to get sick a lot and get fired. Please, I'm sorry! Please don't hit me again; my face and head still hurt."

But Uncle Abe continued to administer his brand of punishment again and again across her face and head. Sarah watched, and felt helpless.

He picked up her Social Studies book and threw it at the mirror over the dresser. The mirror shattered, scattering seven more years of bad luck over the floor. The book knocked her doll off the dresser and pieces of its porcelain head landed on the ground. The broken face stared as Uncle Abe punched the girl in the right eye and threatened to smash her nose and teeth.

The wails grew louder. The aunt and cousin rushed in to avert further damage. They tried to stop the enraged man. The girl fought back, but her uncle, stronger and larger, pressed harder and tighter around her neck. She gasped for breath, becoming dizzy as the oxygen lost its way to her brain. She hung like a ragdoll in her uncle's grip.

51

After Abe realized what he had done, he sat on the bed next to his niece's dead body and shouted, "What the hell am I going to do now?" He buried his head in his hands and cried as Aunt Grace cradled Allie in her arms, asking Jesus and her sister for forgiveness. Mikey stood alone by the doorway, taking everything in without saying a word.

Sarah awoke with a jolt. The dream shocked her, but she knew it had already happened and couldn't be undone. How strange, she thought, that the layout of the bedroom so closely resembled her own bedroom in the apartment on Kingsbridge Avenue. She recalled the other dreams—the similarities between her old apartment, the building's hallway, and her old neighborhood. All of these parallels convinced her that she had lived in Allie's apartment, and that she must bring Allie's story back to life. But for now she resisted. She rolled over and fell into slumber; this time, deeper than before.

*

Sarah returned to the dream, alone with Allie, who was no longer dead and bore no scars from the beatings. Together, they watched the room fade. All the previous shouting and crying disappeared. A gray-blue mist came into view as the mystery developed—the fog and flora illuminated in multiple shades of grays and blues. Sarah couldn't tell whether this was the end or the beginning of the day.

They crossed a solitary path into the woods, where everything had been tinted in iridescent gray-blue. Trees and shrubs glowed in the dark, leaves and fruit in full prominence.

52

Flowers and exotic plant life, both real and imagined, blossomed everywhere—a sachet of perfume filled the air: honeysuckle, jasmine, rose, and mimosa. Crickets serenaded as Sarah's nostrils and eyes took pleasure in this Garden of Eden.

Allie moved closer and looked up at Sarah's five-foot, nine-inch frame. Without emotion, Allie took Sarah's hand and together they walked toward a bush in full bloom, resplendent in remarkable orchid-like flowers. The scent was intoxicating, almost narcotic.

At Allie's request, Sarah wore a blindfold, and stepped aside for Sarah to be alone. The pleasant breeze turned cold and the perfumed lair became remnants of stale musk. A familiar sensation beckoned, and Sarah's breasts remembered the excitement. She ripped off her shirt for the chill to excite her areolas—desiring cool fingers, lips, and tongue. Sarah removed her panties. Her vagina wept, and from the bush, her invisible lover heard her and came forth in the flesh. She didn't see his cadaver-like visage as his penis entered her.

Her vagina hurt from the rough penetration, but Sarah got what she wished for. Soaked in sweat and body fluids, she touched herself. Immune to pain, she begged him to remove her blindfold. She squeezed her breasts for her nipples to harden to stone. Sarah remained on her knees and accepted his will to do more.

Allie peeked from behind a nearby tree. She knew this creature with the burnt face and contorted hands. He was the same man in the bushes who lured her to his world and returned to the place where she died in that same Bronx bedroom where Sarah once slept.

Sarah crawled past the broken branches and fallen petals, whimpering like a wounded animal. Her ravished body shook in the passing wind.

The time came to take Sarah back, and Allie dragged her by the legs to the roadway.

She whispered in her ear, "Poor Sarah, I'm sorry for what happened. I'm under orders. If I refuse, I'll get beaten to a pulp. When he was alive, he was a lonely man who never had luck with women. He was an arsonist who burned down his house, killing his mother and accidentally killing himself. That's why he's deformed. He's miserable in the afterlife and seeks revenge by preying on loners like you. What can I say, Sarah! I don't want to be beaten again. My uncle was bad, but this monster is worse. Like me, you must learn to obey. You must fall in love with this pitiful creature, and he will do the same. He needs love, just like you."

Two minutes later, Sarah woke up, swollen and in agony. There was blood on her chest and down her thighs. Her vagina ached and smelled rancid. Her shirt lay next to her, ripped in half, and her panties lay crumpled on the floor.

She wanted to shower. However, all thoughts of cleanliness faded at the sight of herself in the mirror. Scrapes covered her body, and skin and blood crusted underneath her nails. *Had she done this to herself?* Drops of blood, not milk, seeped from her nipples. Frightened, she thought that perhaps she had not caused these wounds. Even worse, she thought she might be in love with him. She put on a clean T-shirt and panties, and went to bed. Her shower would have to wait until morning.

Sarah returned to the dream-state. She stood outside the bathroom, naked, fearing for her safety. She ran over to check the door—it was locked. She threw a towel around her bruised body and checked the windows—they too were locked. She panicked and dialed Jen, but a small hand got in the way.

Allie said, "Sarah, I think we should talk, but first you have to calm down."

Surprised to see Allie again, Sarah was speechless. After a few moments, she regained her senses and said, "Talk? Maybe over milk and cookies? Look at me! I'm covered in scrapes, bruises, and blood. I don't believe I did this to myself. Calm down? You tricked me into performing vile acts. Would these acts be classified as rape? How could I prove it to a doctor or the police? I can't tell anyone about this. Should I tell Jen? Who'd believe me?"

Allie insisted on talking, admonishing Sarah for her refusal to listen. Sarah, in return, ordered her out of the apartment, threatening to beat her, just like her uncle had.

The bathroom door suddenly slammed shut. Sarah opened it, and Allie was gone.

Sarah awakened and sighed with relief. She washed herself, watching the suds swirl clockwise before sliding down the drain. She applied antibacterial cream to the gashes; as she did this, her nipples hardened. She wondered about the dream—was it rape or a sick fantasy, or a nightmare from stress?

Sarah applied makeup, using a concealer to cover up the bags under her eyes. She got dressed and changed the sheets. She tossed them into a garbage bag, along with her shredded, soiled clothes. On her laptop, she dumped Allie's story. Her cramps began to subside. *Writing this novel is a silly pipe dream,* she thought, and then she said *the hell with it.*

Hungry, she craved eggs and sausages at one of the local diners. A generous slice of cherry cheesecake and two cups of coffee would complete a hearty meal. Normally, she would avoid such an extravagant intake of calories, but today she was going to celebrate her freedom from Allie and her disfigured accomplice, and hopefully, from Jill. She would call for the interview after breakfast and then take the train downtown to see a foreign flick at the Angelika Theater. Maybe she would buy new clothes and makeup or get her hair done. The day had many possibilities.

*

Sarah took a chance with Pierre Gautier Cuts, a fast-food type of salon for the budget-conscious, where walk-ins were welcome. The receptionist directed Sarah to Peter, who wasn't busy. Sarah disliked him immediately, but no one else was available, and she needed a new do.

When Peter saw his new customer, he shook his head and bared his pearly grin. His voice was cold. "Good morning, honey. How's life? Are you here to attract a certain somebody?"

Sarah answered, "No, just a trim with layers and highlights for a job interview."

He escorted her to the sink. She stiffened in the chair, stretching her neck backward, waiting for Peter to carry on the conversation during the shampooing. He slapped a towel around her neck and said, "Lean back, please. Time to lather you up."

Sarah complained that the water was too cold. Peter gave an exaggerated apology and adjusted the temperature. However, the towel slid from Sarah's neck, and Peter pretended not to notice, allowing her neck to rest unprotected on the porcelain surface. Sarah said nothing, hoping this experience would be over soon. She soon learned that his bad mood was due to losing out on a job prospect down in SoHo. Yet Sarah found it preferable to listen to his problems than think about her own.

After his rant, he switched the conversation, with Sarah as the focal point. She kept to the basics—she had no boyfriend, she hated her boss, and she couldn't afford to travel. She didn't say a word about her crazy dream escapades with a stranger, deeming it a little too over-the-top.

After towel-drying her hair, Peter escorted Sarah back to the styling chair. He started complaining about his significant other dumping him for a much older and wealthier guy from London. She sat powerless in the chair—her hair, vulnerable to his scathing fits—wondering if Allie had prearranged this ordeal.

Peter picked up his silver shears, ready to operate. He scooped up a handful of hair and sneered, "Look in the mirror, Princess, you have damage here. See? You'll need more than a

57

trim to clean up this mess, love!" His right hand waved her locks like a red flag. In his other hand, the stainless steel blades moved into swift action.

Sarah lowered her head as directed. The scissors, more menacing than before, clipped to the tune of *snip, snip.* Large chunks flew on the floor and into her lap. Alarmed at what he was doing, she shouted for him to stop scalping her.

The hairdresser retorted, "I'm not scalping you, dear! I'm giving you a more professional look. It's only six inches; I left enough hair to frame your face. It's just an inch above your shoulders and will grow out by the fall. Besides, I think this new length makes you look younger. I bet you're pushing forty, yes?"

Sarah yelled, "Forty? I'm nowhere near forty. How dare you insult me like this!"

He lowered his head to her ear level and said, "Honey, are your hormones going postal? If you want to succeed in this dog-eat-dog world, you'd better loosen up! This is Reality101, sweetie! No one gives a shit about you. Maybe if you stop freaking out, you could pass for thirty."

The manager overheard the dispute and asked Peter to see her immediately. After a brief argument, he stormed out of the salon. The manager apologized for Peter's bad behavior and Sarah's shabby hairdo. She corrected the damage by adding layers and threw in complimentary highlights as part of the peace package. Sarah left the salon looking like a model.

She passed by a new boutique, Josephine's Couture, and admired the black suit on display. The suit was both professional-looking and sexy. Ms. Johnson, the overzealous sales associate, rushed into the fitting room without knocking, holding a size eight black suit for Sarah. Sarah's scraped-up body made her gasp.

"Here's the last one in your size," said Ms. Johnson. Trying hard not to look shocked, the sales associate quietly backed out of the fitting room and left her embarrassed customer alone.

Relieved, Sarah closed the curtain and tried on the size eight. The suit fit her perfectly. After reading the tag—$350— she hesitated, but convinced herself that this purchase would not go to waste.

The sales associate rang up the sale on Sarah's MasterCard. She packed the purchase in pink paper and inserted it in a glossy white shopping bag. With a slight smile, Ms. Johnson handed the shopping bag to Sarah and wished her a nice day.

Sarah reciprocated with the same line, noting concern in the associate's blue eyes. She took the package, certain that she saw Allie by the fitting room, dressed in her blue and white dress, smiling back at her. After putting away her credit card, Sarah looked again, but the child had mysteriously vanished. Sarah left the boutique, fearing that she would never be free from Allie.

Chapter 5

Sarah
(2001)

On Thursday morning, Sarah ran up the subway stairs at 60th Street and Lexington Avenue. Due to a sick passenger, she was running late for her 9:30 interview with the creative director, Jackie Friedman, at Focus NYC. Sweat streaked her eye shadow and the June heat wave targeted her for a bad hair day. The length wasn't to her liking. Her blonde highlighted strands were scattered and some stuck to her forehead. Her head could pass for a haystack.

At the corner of 58th Street, she waited for the light. An impatient taxi made a sharp right at the corner, almost knocking her down. She cursed the inattentive driver, but the cabbie just drove on. Sarah readjusted her mindset and hurried down the block to her destination.

Architecturally splendid, the brick and glass edifice intimidated and dwarfed the tall job applicant as she pushed the revolving door that led to the air-conditioned lobby. She crossed her fingers in silent prayer, fixing her hair in the lobby's mirrored walls by the security desk. The clock above the guard's head read 9:11.

Sarah stuttered, "Fo-Focus NYC, please. My name's Sar-Sarah Kahn. I'm here for an interview with Jackie Friedman at 9:30."

The burly security guard dialed Jackie Friedman's secretary and announced Sarah's arrival. He instructed her to take the elevator on the left and go up to the fifth floor. Then he whispered *good luck* and gave her a wink.

Sarah thanked him and headed toward the elevators. She saw people boarding and called out for someone to hold the elevator. The passengers ignored her, and the doors closed in Sarah's face. She pressed the button and had to wait several minutes for the next one.

When the elevator came, several people squeezed into the car. A man got off on 2, and two women engaged in loud conversation casually exited on 3. The fourth floor received three more passengers in exchange for two. The elevator bypassed the fifth floor, and three men got off on 7. At that point, Sarah realized that she had forgotten to press her floor, and pressed the number 5 button several times. Alone, she stared at her distorted image in the security mirror above. Her watch read 9:28. When she exited the elevator on the fifth floor, she inhaled extra air for courage before opening the glass door.

Sarah introduced herself to the perky twenty-something receptionist and told her she had a 9:30 appointment to see Ms. Friedman. The receptionist told her to take a seat, before letting Jackie know that Sarah was there.

Sarah thanked her and sat down on the long blue sofa. After twenty-two minutes, the receptionist called Ms. Friedman again and reminded her that Sarah was still waiting.

Now the smiling receptionist informed Sarah that she could see Ms. Friedman in the office two doors to the left. She wished Sarah good luck and told her not to worry—*just smile and think positive.*

Sarah had heard that clichéd advice a thousand times before and hoped that she hadn't jinxed herself by ditching *The Allie Chronicles.*

Jackie Friedman, a stylish woman in her mid-thirties with short black hair, stood waiting outside her office doorway. She greeted Sarah and escorted her inside.

"Hello, Sarah! I'm sorry I was detained. I had a long-distance call from Dallas. You know the drill. Anyway, you look fabulous! I love your hair! Did you lose weight? What gym do you hang out at? Are you on the Atkins Diet?"

Sarah shook her head no.

"Sit down, Sarah, and make yourself comfortable. So, it's been five years since we last saw each other, but I never forget super people like you. I'll ask Carol to order some coffee and muffins. Are you scheduled to return to Steinberger's?"

Sarah answered, "No, Jackie, I took the day off. Thanks again for remembering me. You look fantastic too. You're still the First Lady of Style. Stress and budget keep me trim, jogging from one problem to another. I needed a makeover and here I am, blonde and ready to roll. By the way, here's my portfolio and a few samples written for Andy Zarelli when I . . ."

"How's life treating you lately?" interrupted Jackie. Her tone was suddenly cutting edge. Through her red glasses, she scrutinized the applicant, while flipping through the portfolio in a perfunctory manner. "And how are things at Steinberger's?"

Sarah lied and said that everything was fine.

Jackie eyed her and said, "I do have a position available here in our Fashion Division, but I'm curious to know why you didn't apply for another position at Steinberger's." She flipped through the portfolio again and her calculating brown irises eyed Sarah up and down.

Sarah took a deep breath and replied, "As a matter of fact, I applied here at Focus a few months ago and would have been placed had Andy stayed on. He really liked my portfolio. I wrote a few ads for him, as you can see." She pulled out five Christmas campaign ads. "He left for the West Coast last year and, unfortunately, passed away several months ago, from AIDS."

"Hmmm," said Jackie. "How do you and Jill Myers get along?" Jackie looked straight into Sarah's puzzled hazel eyes, ready to probe deeper.

Sarah hesitated slightly, claiming that she and Jill got along just fine. She wondered why Jackie was interrogating her like a witness to a crime, and now she was convinced that dumping the Allie files had not been such a good idea. The creative director's dagger-like eyes made her nervous.

Jackie moved in a little closer and said, "Sarah, I need someone who is ambitious, as well as outgoing. This person must be even-tempered and a team player. Sarah, I really like you and commend you for trying so hard. But in this competitive market, I need a person who is not only qualified but can grow with the changing times. You did all that, but stopped after Mr. Zarelli left the company. If you wanted to be a writer so badly, why didn't you pursue it earlier? You could have partnered with Jill. It surprises me to hear you say that you and she get along just fine. My hunch is that you have a problem with her."

Sarah stood up and said, "Excuse me? What does Jill Myers have to do with my ability to write? You're the one who praised me when I did temp work here back in '95. And here's your letter encouraging me to call you for an interview!"

Sarah tossed the letter on the desk and added, "I don't understand why you arranged for this interview when you had qualms about hiring me."

Jackie intended to end the interview as a peacemaker. In a low voice, she addressed Sarah. "Look, don't give up! A calm demeanor is a sign of maturity and professionalism—a requirement for any job that you might hold throughout your career. I suggest that you seek out a job counselor and try to improve some of the negative aspects of your personality. Talent is not enough, nor is a makeover going to guarantee you a successful interview or a new job."

Sarah's ego plummeted and her precious work lay wasted on top of her black portfolio. A coffin would have been more appropriate. She tossed the once-priceless piece of paper into the wastepaper basket.

Jackie zipped Sarah's portfolio shut and handed it back to her. She extended her hand, a gesture implying that the interview was over.

Sarah gave her a cold nod and reciprocated with a final handshake. She clutched her portfolio and responded accordingly. "Jackie, I'm sorry about my little outburst, but whatever goes on between Jill and me is personal. Thank you for your time, and I will certainly consider your advice."

Jill softened her tone. "Sarah, give it some thought. Think of today as a valuable lesson. We all make mistakes and it's up to us to move on in order to achieve our goals. Good luck to you, and do keep in touch."

Sarah exited in silence. Jackie watched her disappear from view and checked the door, making sure it would lock before closing it. She returned to her high-back leather chair, and dialed.

"Hi, Jill, it's Jackie Friedman. Yes, I kept Sarah waiting while you and I had that long chat. Ha ha. You really described her to a T. That defensive attitude is something else. I thought that maybe she'd grown out of it, but she hasn't changed a bit, although she does look good with her new hairstyle and black suit. Personally, I think she needs a hot date to straighten her out. Maybe you can fix her up with your ex from Stanford Associates? That investment banker with the big attitude and big *you know what*?"

"Not him! You've got to be kidding," chuckled Jill.

The phone rang and the laughter was put on hold. Jackie had a brief conversation with the receptionist before returning to the Gentlewomen's Agreement.

"Wait, Jill. My new receptionist, Carol, just informed me that Brent MacDonald is waiting outside for his 10:30 interview."

Jill said, "Hey, don't worry about it; I have to make it sound legit. Tell your sister, Melissa, that her boyfriend's pal from college is hired. Stop it! I'll be a good girl and won't rob the cradle. Let's celebrate over a few Cosmopolitans tonight at the Union Square Café at seven, maybe eight? It would be nice if Melissa could join us."

*

Sarah would have said what she was thinking, but business etiquette trumped emotion. As she rushed toward the reception area, she dropped her portfolio. A brown-haired man with a Palm Pilot quickly retrieved it. He smiled and said, "Pardon me, I think this is yours?"

Wondering what else could go wrong today, Sarah gave a brusque thank you.

"Hey, what's the hurry? My name is Brent MacDonald. Here's my card. Call me on my cell phone. I'd like to get together with you later on, let's say, seven o'clock at P.J. Clarke's, over on 55th and Third. It would be cool to have a chat over a few drinks."

She accepted the card without saying thank you.

66

As Sarah headed for the exit, the receptionist whispered, "How did it go?"

"Fine, just fine," she snapped as she turned away. The receptionist read her body language and refrained from delving further. Sarah said goodbye and pulled the glass door open. She escaped, taking large strides to the elevators.

But Brent beat her there. An empty elevator arrived, and he noted her sour expression but persisted and held the doors open. He was used to getting what he wanted, and he wasn't going to let this elusive blonde fly away. Finally, she divulged her name, abruptly, claiming that she had another appointment.

"Busy bees on the run must make time for fun," said Brent. "Tonight at seven, please. We can do dinner afterward if you'd like, Sarah Kahn. Are you game for my game plan?" His eyes met hers and he winked for emphasis—the second wink of the day.

Cornered by the good-looking wolf in business attire, she was lured into his trap, ignoring the threat of more bad luck in one day from Allie's curse. Before boarding the elevator, she reluctantly agreed to go on a date with him. He smiled as the elevator doors closed.

Brent returned to his seat in the reception area. The phone rang, and the receptionist motioned to Brent that Ms. Friedman would see him now, and wished him good luck.

In return, he said, *"Grazie, Signorina Carol.* I hope your trip to Rome will be fun. *Ciao! A presto!"*

67

He strolled into Jackie's office, a perfect portrait of confidence. She welcomed him like an old friend and gave him the red carpet treatment, ushering him to the chair that had recently been occupied by Sarah.

Jackie said, "Well hello, Brent. Ready for some good news? You're hired! Welcome to Focus NYC! Oh, before I forget, here's your portfolio." She handed him the initialed portfolio as if it were a present. "It reveals your personality— energetic, dynamic, and forward-thinking. You're absolutely suited for the job, and I'm so glad my sister has such great taste when it comes to selecting the right man."

Brent asked her when his new job would start. His perfect smile convinced Jackie that she would eventually have him under her coverlet.

She grinned, permitting him to peek at her slightly crooked bottom teeth. She knew that her new subordinate was aware that he was under her control, and she loved it—as if she were a junior at Boston University again. Hoping he could start next Monday, she asked him when he could leave Patterson and Peters.

Brent interjected that he had to give his two weeks' notice first but asked if Jackie could give him a sneak preview of his new office.

"Shit, that damn two weeks' notice. I guess I'll have to be patient. Okay, Brent, have it your way this time," giggled his new boss. "Let me be your tour guide for today. As it happens, your cubicle is not far from my office. And, by the way, feel free to ask me any questions."

Brent smiled and extended his hand to seal the deal. She offered hers out of custom. His strong grip seduced her. She subdued herself behind business casual. He exited first, leaving traces of Armani as a tease.

She introduced Brent to one of her assistant fashion writers, a red-headed woman in her twenties named Nicole Van Meers. Brent charmed Nicole with a warm handshake and flirty eye contact. Nicole smiled, but she too was restricted by business decorum—this was not the time for Happy Hour behavior.

Upon leaving, Brent grinned like a Cheshire cat, marking his new territory with his Armani scent. He boarded the elevator, raising the eyebrows of two female passengers. His mind turned to that uptight blonde—her body heat and Dior perfume left on the upholstery. Like Julius Caesar, he came, he saw, and he would conquer Ms. Sarah Kahn, the Iron Maiden. A few drinks at P.J.'s might melt her tonight.

Chapter 6

Sarah
(2001)

In her kitchen, Sarah examined Brent's card by the light over the sink. The bold, black Century Gothic lettering on white captivated her, but she still felt irritated about having lost out on the job, and her excitement over having a date with a nice-looking guy presented a conundrum: *Would he be overly assertive over drinks and dinner—what would happen when wine turned the conversation toward sex—how would he react if she refused to have sex with him on the first date—should she tell him that she was still a virgin?*

Despite her trepidation, she planned to meet him at seven. She still had time to shower and redo her makeup. She touched up her hair and spritzed herself with Diorissimo perfume. She would put on her new black dress, adding pearls for a classic look. Despite the botched interview, she looked good. She wondered whether she was being too judgmental about her date. Maybe he could assist her in getting a job elsewhere. She couldn't ask Jen for her opinion, since Jen had stopped returning her calls. Her sales position at *The New Yorker* had transformed her into a stranger. *The hell with her*, Sarah thought.

*

Bent checked his Rolex watch. The last-minute meeting for the Pepsi account wouldn't be over for at least another half hour—the Pepsi account executive was arguing over the cost of re-shooting the commercial. Luckily, Patterson and Peters Associates was located only two blocks south of P.J. Clarke's, but Brent had no way of contacting the bar, as his boss frowned on the use of cell phones during meetings. Besides, Sarah hadn't offered her phone number and was probably on the way. He hoped she wouldn't be too annoyed at his tardiness and disappear before 7:30.

*

The entrance to P.J. Clarke's was brimming with hotshot execs. Sarah canvassed the predominantly male bastion. In this revved-up milieu, elevator eyes searched for potential scores and testosterone craved a late-night romp on two-hundred-thread sheets. Most girls went to bars in pairs. Alone, Sarah nervously walked past the queue of loud men, searching for Brent. It was 7:01, and he was nowhere in sight. The smoke in the room irritated her—early warning signs of a bad date. She believed that The Fates must have teamed up with Allie. At 7:15, Sarah waited at the bar, but Brent was still not there. She hated being stood up and decided to leave. But someone caught her in the act.

A man's voice said, "Hey, honey, why the glum look? I've been watching you for the past fifteen minutes and now you're running out? Were you stood up? Well, life ain't fair, and here is a lovely lady alone without a drink. What would you like, sweetheart? You look like a Cosmopolitan girl. My name's Eddie. What's yours?"

Sarah turned her head to locate the face belonging to the thick Queens accent. A balding, potbellied, middle-aged man lifted his Heineken beer to her. *Shit, always the desperados. Where the hell is Brent?*

Eddie cornered her and said, "Hey, sweetheart, why the panic? I don't bite on the first date, ha ha. I ain't no vampire, although I am half Romanian. The other part of me's Irish. I'm a smart and sensitive Scorpio, a very single Catholic forty-three-year-old going on twenty-nine. I'm an accountant who's looking for love and companionship, not like these jerks here. Are you waiting for someone? Someone who's obviously a no-show."

"I'm not here to listen to your personal ad, Eddie," snapped Sarah. "My date is late, and I wish you'd leave me alone! I think you're more interested in your Heineken than in the women here."

Eddie cleared his throat for the counterattack. "Well, you can't judge a book by its cover. That's the problem with most of you girls today. Looking for a handsome prince with money and a fast lay, and see what happens? You need to kiss a few frogs if you want somebody who's not celluloid. I can see that you're not from a well-to-do background. You try too hard to impress with your clothes and hair but lack the social skills that go with them. Honey, we can't always get what we want. Loosen up, sweetie.

72

You might even learn to have a good time before you're over the hill, or maybe you already are?"

"Hey, Eddie, I told you that my date is late and I wish to be left alone. Do I have to call the cops?"

"Hey, Eddie, you heard the lady. Now move back to your corner and behave," interrupted Brent. His athletic hand slapped Eddie on the back.

Sarah watched the Scorpion stallion lose his sting and retreat back to his Heineken. The bottle had a feminine quality—a slender neck and full bottom—perhaps an adequate substitute for her. The frog couldn't defend himself against the handsome prince. Eddie's eyes met Sarah's, and she nervously looked away.

Brent turned toward his date and said, "Sorry I'm late, Sarah. I was detained at a meeting."

Sarah looked upset, and Brent surmised that Mr. Loudmouth was the culprit. He asked if she was all right and offered to take her somewhere else. She nodded, and he escorted her out, leaving Eddie to nurse his grievance over another beer.

He hailed a cab and gave the address of a quiet French bistro ensconced in his TriBeCa neighborhood. When the cabbie stopped for a red light at the corner of Chambers Street, Brent observed his date. She was tall, slim, and attractive, and her black dress and simple strand of pearls gave her a sophisticated look.

Sarah wondered how Brent perceived her. Did he think she was passive-aggressive, nervous, or lacked social skills? Did

73

he pick up on her being shy or having deep-rooted problems with men?

The cab stopped in front of the tiny restaurant, Le Chat Noir. Brent held the door for Sarah to exit and then held the door for Sarah to enter the restaurant. He glanced at his Rolex watch. It was almost eight. He wondered if he had made a mistake asking her out but was willing to see how the night developed.

Brent greeted the maître d' in French. *"Bonsoir, Georges, ça va? Une table pour deux, s'il vous plaît."*

"Bonsoir, Madam et Monsieur. Par ici, s'il vous plaît."

"Oui, merci," replied Brent, slipping a folded bill into the maître d's pocket. Brent didn't have to make a reservation, since he was friendly with the owner.

The hushed atmosphere and obsequious treatment from the restaurant staff amused Sarah. She concealed her enthusiasm, noticing her date's slightly irked expression. Was she overdoing the phrase *thank you very much?*

"This way, Sarah," smiled Brent, and she walked beside him to their table by the mural of Toulouse-Lautrec's Paris.

This time she whispered one *thank you* to the maître d', who pulled the chair out for her. Brent nodded approvingly and took his seat. The waiter handed him the menu and, on cue, recited the specials of the day.

Pressure knitted a knot in her stomach. The whole evening felt rehearsed. Sarah felt out of place dining at a fine restaurant with Brent. The oysters and wine weren't agreeing with her, and her fancy entrée was still in the oven. Sarah sensed

74

that Brent liked being in control. He had self-assurance and money to back him up. She sat without flexing a muscle, listening to him recount his achievements from his college days, and his ski trips to Vail and Aspen, and snorkeling down in the Virgin Islands. Sarah felt like nothing more than an office worker with new clothes covering up a vacant life.

The waiter came back with a folding stand and set it up before Sarah and Brent. He presented the entrées. Pleased with the nouvelle cuisine, Brent encouraged his reluctant date to have a taste of his braised venison.

He said, "Come, dear—uh, no pun intended," and offered her a bite from his fork. "Isn't it good? Allow me to taste this delightful mushroom soufflé, if you're not eating it."

Sarah's teeth chewed the meat slowly, and she imagined herself as Nora Helmer from Henrik Ibsen's *A Doll's House*. She hated eating the flesh of Rudolph's cousin; however, she feigned obedience, since he would be paying the bill.

Brent laughed and said, "If you're a vegetarian, I promise not to shoot you," and squeezed her hand.

She pierced the large dome of her soufflé. The heat sizzled out, releasing the delicious scent of mushrooms, eggs, and cheese. "Wow, this is awesome," exclaimed Sarah. She offered him the first bite, but it missed his mouth and dropped into his plate.

Brent smiled and retrieved the morsel, resuming the conversation while Sarah hunted for mushrooms. He bragged non-stop about his work accomplishments, and then he shifted the conversation to his new job at Focus NYC.

To Sarah, the words felt like a slap, and she interrupted him mid-sentence. "Excuse me, what did you say about a new job at Focus NYC?"

"I said that I was hired by Jackie Friedman. I'm her new fashion copywriter." His grin widened to expose his perfect Trident teeth.

Suddenly feeling like the main character in *Alice in Wonderland*, Sarah metaphorically shrank, but it wasn't the mushrooms that were responsible; she blamed it on the man sitting across from her, smiling as he cut another slice of medium-rare venison. *It might as well be my heart,* she thought dramatically, watching the blood ooze on the plate, clotting with raspberry wine sauce. She looked down at her plate and said nothing, her knife and fork motionless, the soufflé losing its appeal.

Brent extended his hand to her, inquiring if she was okay, thinking that perhaps the soufflé was too rich for her. He offered to order her a ginger ale. Sarah refused to answer at first, but then admitted that her stomach felt queasy and she wanted to go home.

Brent offered to call for a cab to take her home. He even suggested that she rest up for a few hours in his apartment nearby, where she could take some Pepto-Bismol and he could make her some chamomile tea.

Her hazel eyes narrowed as she said, "Brent, don't blame the soufflé for messing up my stomach. It's hearing about your good news. I was interviewed for that position today and was rejected by the woman who hired you. I did freelance work for her in 1995. She loved my work and asked me to stay in touch. Today, she shredded my dignity. Then you came along and *bingo*—so obviously prearranged! Thank you very much, Mr. Trust Fund Kid MacDonald. Sorry for my lack of savoir faire. There's an expression that people from my background use— *money talks, shit walks*. Oh, by the way, don't forget to zip your fly the next time you leave the restroom."

Sarah's crumpled napkin fell to the floor, leaving a faint scent of her perfume as she bolted from the table.

"Why not say it louder for the entire restaurant to hear! Ms. Kahn, thank you very much for your charming company," shouted Brent.

He looked down, his face turning the color of the wine sauce in his plate as he hurried off to the men's room. The women at the next table couldn't control their laughter. Their girls' night out had just gotten better.

Brent returned a minute later, and the maître d' asked, "Is everything all right, *Monsieur*?"

"The check, Georges. Give me the goddamn check!"

Chapter 7

Sarah
(2001)

After Sarah stormed out of the restaurant, Brent paid the bill and apologized to the maître d' for the unfortunate confrontation with his date. He needed the cool summer night air to relieve his pique, so instead of taking a cab he walked to his apartment near Duane Street. His father had warned him about these lower-class girls in the business world—they lacked the sophistication and the right genetics for breeding. Brent had argued back, stating that anyone could elevate themselves in society, and how many millionaires in the U.S.A. had started from humble beginnings. However, these battles always ended in a draw. Tonight, though, Brent had gotten a firsthand taste of class agitation, conceding that his getting a coveted job over a woman struggling up the ladder of success was due to socioeconomic privilege. He felt sorry for Sarah and intended to call her later to apologize and ask her how she was feeling. After all, poor Sarah lived outside of Manhattan and had to travel a long distance to Queens via subway.

*

The phone's incessant ringing annoyed Sarah. Like the train on her trip home, her keys took a long time to do their job, but then, *abracadabra,* the door finally opened. She zoomed inside, dropping her bag and its contents. She slipped on a rolling lipstick case, almost twisting her right ankle. She grabbed the receiver and mumbled *hello.*

"Sarah, it's Brent."

"Yes, Brent," she answered in a snide voice. *Why did I give this jerk my home number? What a dumb thing to do! Now, how do I get rid of him?*

Brent said, "Look, honey, I want to talk to you about tonight."

"Yes, Brent. Do you want me to say I'm sorry for my bad behavior after being screwed out of a job by the guy at my table, or should I rephrase it and say *your* table?"

"Whoa, Sarah, I called to say I'm sorry about this misunderstanding," replied Brent. "I had no idea you were being interviewed for the same job."

"Yeah, right! Do you have friends or family in the business? Based on Jackie's previous feedback, I thought I had my foot in the door, but today you came to Focus NYC and slammed that door on my foot. It hurts to have one's pride stepped on by people at work, but especially by an outsider who took what should have been mine."

Brent held his breath and apologized for the coincidence of both of them applying for the same position.

She hung up without a comment or goodbye, leaving Brent in a one-way conversation. The phone rang again for Sarah's answering machine to record Brent's plea for forgiveness, but *forgiveness* had dropped out of Sarah's vocabulary.

She went to the bathroom for ibuprofen to relieve her worsening headache. After doing her nightly wash-up, she headed for the bedroom and entered the dreamscape.

*

In the dream, Sarah was washing her hands, when a small hand tapped her wrist. It was Allie.

Allie grabbed Sarah by the hand and said, "Sarah, we must settle something if you want to live to see tomorrow. I'm not kidding. My attacker means business. For thirty-five years, I'm a woman trapped in a child's body."

"Get away from me before I call the cops," shouted Sarah. She panicked, wondering, Am I going crazy? Maybe it's the wine.

"Sarah, you know you can't do that. Take a look in the mirror. Whose reflection do you see?"

Dumbfounded, she listened, forgetting that she was dreaming. There was no evidence of a ten-year-old in the bathroom mirror. She saw only her own distraught face.

Allie apologized for what had happened, swearing that she didn't know that the deformed man would assault Sarah. Perhaps he had picked up mournful vibes in the place where Allie had died.

Sarah lost her speech, and in spite of the ibuprofen, her headache became unbearable.

Allie proceeded to make predictions about Brent MacDonald, and Sarah's former roommates, Kate Robbins and Dana Chu. Brent would be promoted to Jackie's position when Jackie left to start her own agency in L.A. in two months. Kate Robbins, who worked at Estée Lauder, would be hired to work for Brent at Focus NYC. Jackie would ask a friend to hire Brent as the copy director at her new agency, Jennings, Holmes and Rogers Associates, near Wall Street. Dana Chu would move to Brooklyn and open a boutique there. She added that the nameless creature that Sarah had met in her sleep planned to beat Allie, and Allie needed Sarah's help. "Give him what he needs. Write my story. It will help you out financially—and set us both free from our unhappiness."

Allie massaged Sarah's shoulder, kissing her cheeks while singing a hypnotic melody to relax her. The child took her hand and led her to the bedroom. She clicked on Sarah's laptop and showed Sarah that the story had, in fact, not been trashed; a duplicate copy had been misfiled in her photos folder.

Sarah's face froze. There it was, her Times New Roman words recounting Allie's horrific tale. She lowered her head and let Allie's hand pull her arm.

Sarah awakened on the toilet set, still dressed in the outfit she had worn on her ill-fated date. She cleaned up and went into the bedroom to check her computer files. Allie was right; a duplicate was indeed sitting in her photos folder. Stunned by the dream, Sarah lay on her bed and wept until she fell asleep again.

Moonlight cast a gray-blue light onto the keyboard. Sarah lay in her bed, motionless. Allie kissed her head and tiptoed away from the bed. An exchange of whispers took place with someone outside the bedroom. Sarah heard Allie say, "Don't worry, I have her confidence again." Allie tiptoed back to her. The whispers persisted, and Sarah deciphered Allie's final message: "She's at peace now. See how lovely she looks."

The scene shifted and Sarah was back in the forest— unafraid and at peace—stronger and more willing to face her abuser again. Physical beauty belonged to show-off men like Brent. She forgave the creature for the pain that he had inflicted upon her. She wanted to make peace with him and move on with her life. Her breasts ached because her hormones were in flux.

She ripped open the front of her dress, happily watching the onyx-like buttons cascade. No longer sewn to fabric, each button rolled to new places. She did the same with the strand of pearls, which had been a gift from her parents when she graduated from college. She discarded her watch, earrings, and rings, once cherished, into the pond. The smell of honeysuckle, rose, jasmine, and mimosa scintillated—a familiar scent in familiar scenery shrouded in gray-blue mystery. The air exhilarated her as she removed her dress, tossing it into the pond. She kicked off her shoes and ripped off her pantyhose and undergarments, flinging them all into the water. She smiled, watching them float away. She declared her freedom—a nymph reborn. She caught her image in the pond, observing how

82

beautiful and unflawed she was. She squeezed her remarkably
unscarred breasts, now plump with milk and love. A few drops
flowed from each nipple.

In the distance, Sarah heard the rustling of branches.
The aromas of the forest overwhelmed her as the gray-blue cloud
got darker. A strong wind preceded the lightning that severed the
contorted tree. The tree burst into flames—its sap drenched in
blood, as the tree burned, unconsumed by the flames. Etched in
ugliness, the creature's face now turned erotic and his eyes
became gentle. Sarah's screams reverberated like thunder and
the cloud released the rain. Then the storm subsided into a
gentle rainfall that became a lullaby, and the forest fell asleep.

Sarah awakened—happy, free, and unscathed from her
encounter, with her clothes and jewelry still intact. She had made
peace with the creature, and she would write that book—not
now, but much later, when she was ready. Both she and he had
gotten what they wanted—they had great sex.

Chapter 8

Kate
(2001)

Brent liked making fast strides in life, and networking through Jackie Friedman facilitated his success in just a few months. Thanks to Jackie's connections, Brent acquired a position as the new copy director for Jennings, Holmes and Rogers Associates, and was enjoying the power that came with his title. Conversely, weeding out the résumés for the associate fashion copywriter position took too much of his time, and he dialed his secretary, Christy Sinclair, for assistance.

"No problem," she cooed. Her body heat sent non-work-related messages. Her boss skied and loved mountains, even better, on women.

Twenty-two candidates with their lives condensed on paper awaited promise or rejection. Only a few lucky ones would be called for an interview, while most of the candidates would get 'active file' letters. Instead of starting at the top, Christy pulled one from the bottom and handed it to him.

Brent showed interest. "Hmm, check this one out. Kate Robbins from Focus NYC. I believe she was one of my writers—ambitious, sharp, and smart, as I recall. Let's give her a shot. She's a hard worker and a quick learner; she used to work for Estée Lauder. I see that she's moved to Brooklyn; in fact, to

Park Slope, an up-and-coming neighborhood. Christy, call her for an interview and back it up with a letter from me. Check my calendar first and please finish sorting through the batch, just in case she's not available for the position. Thanks."

He handed her the résumé, and she approved his choice. She knew that her boss would be fair and honor his word. She thanked God for her recent transfer to the Copy Division, and away from the PR Division and Ms. Nanette Darcy, Satan's dominatrix in stiletto heels.

Christy sashayed out the door to make the call. Although at work, her mind wanted to play. Still vibrant at forty-seven, she didn't want sex with some Viagra addict, who in a few years would wear a pacemaker and Depends, and babble about his aches and pains and Social Security. She dialed the work number listed on Ms. Robbins's résumé.

When Kate picked up the phone, Christy said, "Hello, Ms. Robbins. This is Ms. Sinclair from Jennings, Holmes and Rogers Associates. We are pleased to inform you that we have an opening for an interview next Tuesday at ten with Mr. MacDonald for the associate fashion copywriter position. Would that be convenient for you?"

Kate answered, "Yes, I will be available. Thank you, Ms. Sinclair, for getting back to me, and have a nice day."

After hanging up, Kate jumped up and down, chanting *yes! yes! yes!* How lucky that she had kept in touch with Brent. Jen had said that, eventually, good things would happen, and the Ouija board was right.

85

Unlike most office workers, who thought of freedom from paperwork, phone calls, and emails on a Friday night, Kate's mind concentrated on her interview with Brent. The R train to Brooklyn came on time, and in less than forty-five minutes she arrived at Union Street Station. Once above ground, she hummed all the way to her apartment on the third floor of a dove-gray brownstone. Her roommate, Anne Saunders, had taken off for a two-week vacation in Italy, and now Kate had carte blanche to privacy in 3B. Working for Brent would mean being able to rent an apartment without a roommate within a year or less. Another promotion could mean owning a condo. She smiled as she unlocked the front door.

Her old roommate, Dana Chu, an athletic and pretty gal of Ashkenazi, Kenyan, Peruvian, and Chinese descent, had advised her to move to Garfield Place. Dana, who was now her second-floor neighbor, waved to her in the hallway. Eagerly, she tried to talk her into hanging out at one of the new places along Fifth, but Kate politely refused, claiming exhaustion. Out of superstition, she resisted the urge to tell Dana about her upcoming job interview—why risk spoiling her good luck? Her neighbor smiled and said, "Maybe tomorrow?"

They agreed to meet at seven and exchanged 'good nights,' as Dana's door closed and Kate's unlocked.

Kate threw her bag on the chair, went to the closet, and pulled the Ouija board down from the second shelf. It had been Jen's Halloween present when Jen, Kate, Dana, and Sarah shared the apartment on Kingsbridge Avenue in the Bronx. Kate had

86

found this apartment through Dana and wanted Jen, her best friend at Focus NYC, to join her, but Jen made her stay brief, preferred living in a cramped studio off Central Park, up in the West Seventies. She loved the area and the status of the location.

Kate had severed herself from the dating scene—bad luck and too many compromises. She believed her life paralleled Sarah's. Bad karma haunted Sarah, and some of Sarah's bad karma had rubbed off on her. When it came to men, money, virginity, and looks, she still thought of Sarah. Kate debated whether she should keep in touch with Sarah, despite the fact that Sarah never returned Kate's calls or emails. Kate figured that Dana had probably thrown out Sarah's number when she moved here. Jen had worked with Sarah and found her a bit backward and shy. Getting a job at *The New Yorker* had made it easier for her to drop the friendship.

Looking at the tan and black board, she recalled when she and Jen placed their fingertips on the cream-colored plastic. Minutes passed and the disk wouldn't budge. Kate declared the device a hoax, while Jen protested that it had worked before. Kate asked Dana to give it a try. When the same thing happened, Kate asked Sarah to join in.

Sarah reluctantly placed her fingers on the disk. The disk moved slowly and stopped. Jen complained that Sarah had moved it, but Sarah denied it. Another argument ensued, and Kate took Jen's place. This time, the disk was stationary. Sarah suggested that they try it in her room. Jen agreed and placed the board on Sarah's divan. The ritual began—first, Jen with Sarah

87

and then with Kate—both resulted in rapid movement across the black alphabet, making an exit to *GOODBYE*. No one could decipher the message, except for Kate. She testified that she saw the name *ALLIE*.

At first, they argued among themselves—*you pushed it*—*no, you did*. After several sessions, they all concurred that their fingers barely did anything, because the disk had flown across the letters. Something in Sarah's room controlled the board.

The women asked: *Will I get married, will he be rich?*—*How many children will I have?*—*Will I find a new job?*—*I's* dominated All Hallows' Eve. They knew the dead roamed the earth this day and carried messages for the living.

The pin moved to either *YES, NO,* or the numbers—the girls shrieked when the year for Sarah to find love was 2001. She just brushed it off as nonsense, since the disk went to *GOODBYE* for all the other questions. According to the Ouija board, Kate, Jen, and Dana were all slated for new jobs. Nonetheless, the answers for love drifted to *GOODBYE*—so disappointing! The board's activity eventually diminished, as well as all interest and concentration on the part of the girls. They moved on to wine and snacks.

Kate still kept in touch with Jen, who left Steinberger's to work in sales at *The New Yorker*. Jen purchased a pricey condo near Lincoln Center and wore an engagement ring given to her by Steven Fein, an M.D. with a promising future in reconstructive surgery. Their wedding date was set for October

14th. Ms. Olsen planned to trade in her Lutheran name and faith. The board goofed on Jen, claiming that she would never find a man. The board predicted the same fate for Kate and Dana. Kate wondered if that, too, was a hoax.

When Kate moved to Park Slope, the Ouija board stayed in its box. Temptation enticed her and her fingertips to swing into action. She had never tried doing the Ouija board alone. She took a deep breath, her fingers barely touching the plastic disk. The disk moved across the board, swirling across the alphabet. It slowed down, going from *A* to *L* and back again to *L,* before crossing over to *I,* and stopping on *E.* Kate held her breath—the same name she had seen back in her old apartment. Glued to the heart-shaped device, Kate followed her hands, obeying the spirit called *Allie.* Could this be the little girl she had seen in her dreams? Ever since she moved out of that Bronx apartment, Kate had been the recipient of *The Allie Chronicles* through her strange dreams. Kate kept this bizarre secret from Jen and everyone else, but as a former poet, these dreams fascinated her. She liked to write about them, and Allie insisted that her story had to be written, or something bad would happen to Kate.

Kate attempted to connect with Allie, asking, "Will I get the job at Jennings, Holmes and Rogers?" Her fingers rested on the plastic, waiting for the answer. After several minutes, she wondered if she should have tossed this board out months ago. Suddenly, the disk moved to *NO,* before moving downward to *GOODBYE.* Kate concluded that the Allie dreams were just her imagination on overdrive.

Kate preferred to stay home on this Friday night. She ordered chicken and cashews in garlic sauce from the Chinese take-out nearby. She ate half of it and placed the leftovers in the refrigerator. After a quick shower, she brushed her teeth and threw on a lavender nightie. Once in bed, she turned off the light on her nightstand and fell asleep.

*

Kate dreamt of her old bedroom in the Bronx. However, the furniture wasn't hers. Her bedroom had chunky-looking Mediterranean furniture, a style popular in the '60s. Above the headboard, a movie on the wall revealed two actors engaged in physical activity. Although the images were distorted, as if one were looking through thick glass, Kate could discern that the male and female were having sex. The act was disconcerting— was it sexual?—was it rape? Kate couldn't move her eyes off the wall of non-stop moaning and humping but, mercifully, woke up. Like in the dream, darkness occupied her room, and she turned on the light in an attempt to control her anxiety.

She felt driven to type another chapter yet questioned her relationship to the woman in the dream, the ten-year-old child who spent her afterlife roaming a nocturnal forest, and the deformed man with too much testosterone. The latter looked familiar; he was probably the one who had raped the woman. Was this a psychological manifestation of her problems with men and not settling down to start a family? She consoled herself with the thought that she might have her dream job soon.

90

Kate awakened later that morning feeling more exhausted than before. She lifted her head off her arm, which was still asleep. She shook it to get her circulation moving. According to the alarm clock, it was not quite 3:30. *This story will have to be tweaked another time,* Kate thought, and headed to the bathroom to pee.

Grogginess overpowered her, and she almost fell off the toilet seat. Her panties played tug-of-war with her knees. Luckily, she pulled them down in time. Fatigue tested her nerves again, however, and she fell asleep on the toilet seat.

*

The room morphed, and the bathroom looked like the one she had back in the Bronx, except the tile and fixtures were two generations older. Sensing that she wasn't alone, she pulled up her panties. Allie, in her blue mini-dress with white lace, stood by the sink and watched her flush the water. The girl seemed aggressive, and Kate had to convince herself that this was only a dream.

Allie said, "Kate, the Ouija board isn't the easiest way to communicate." The girl's precocious nature played hardball, and Kate could only say "huh?"

"Yes, Kate, we are in a dream, but it's not just a dream. Hear me out before you jump to conclusions. You're still in grave danger."

"What? What danger? What the hell are you talking about? You must be Allie, right?"

91

"Yes, Kate, and the story that you are writing is my story. The man who lured me away from my new home will harm you, unless you learn to fulfill his desires in order to fulfill your own. The scene above your headboard actually happened. That woman was assaulted by him because she did not listen to me."

Kate yelled, "But what does this have to do with me?"

Allie's piercing eyes fixed on Kate, ready to hypnotize her. She said, "He craves unlucky types. It feeds his ego. I still want to help you, Kate."

Kate's logic returned, thinking that she would be waking up soon. She found it hard to look at Allie's razor-sharp almond-brown eyes.

Uninterrupted, the dream turned into another dream. Kate and Allie sat on a rock in a forest, its foliage lush and dense in the dim light. This was Allie's world, and the creature without a name was its master.

In the distance, orange flames exploded from a leafless tree. Allie held Kate's hand and cajoled her attention away from the hypnotic embers. Kate followed her toward the burning tree. Hot flames licked the sky, and the intense heat caused Kate to perspire. Allie encouraged her to stand before the tree. Sweat poured down Kate's forehead and hair, and saturated her T-shirt, outlining her breasts and navel. Her skin glowed in the orange light. Kate looked down at herself and smiled. Allie acknowledged that Kate looked sensuous and squeezed her hand.

The tree burned on, even though the flames did minimal damage to its bark. It sobbed, shedding blood from its trunk.

Kate wanted to touch the blood, and extended her right hand, but Allie pushed it away.

Out from a nearby bush, a woman crawled on all fours, her face unrecognizable and her body naked, with animal-like scrapes and scabs covering her body. A figure in black pulled her back. The woman cried as thunder rocked the sky. Kate broke away from Allie's grip and touched the tree, leaving the child aghast. She pressed her hand against the hot surface as if to communicate with the tree. A thunderbolt hit the tree, splitting it in two. Kate fell backward, landing on the ground.

She woke up on her bathroom floor. Thunder rattled the windows. Kate rose in pain, her butt and left elbow aching. Luckily, she didn't slam her skull. She swallowed two aspirins with lukewarm tap water. She wrapped a few ice cubes inside a towel and placed the towel on the bruised area. Like the rainstorm, the throbbing eventually subsided, and she crawled under the covers.

Chapter 9

Kate
(2001)

The next morning, Dana joined Kate at the local
Laundromat for laundry and gossip. Kate brought along a recent
issue of *New York* magazine and turned the dog-eared pages. Her
left elbow sported the black-and-blue evidence of her early-
morning flop, but at least her rear end felt less painful.

Kate said, "Hey, Dana, I've gotta stop writing about
Allie! Glad I trashed the Ouija board this morning. Never
should've taken it when I moved here."

Between the wash and spin cycles, Kate read an article
on the latest Brooklyn eateries. The Bistro Saint Michel piqued
her interest, and she imagined herself eating crème brûlée
garnished with lavender. Paul Gaston, the manly owner and chef,
served her at a table done in country French—pale-bone lace
cloth and a splash of colorful daisies and heather inside antique
watering cans. He winked at her, and she blushed. The lavender
accented the caramelized dessert. Kate gave in to her inner
romantic—she heard Malcolm McLaren's *"Je T'aime . . . Moi
Non Plus."* Her vagina moistened like lip gloss.

Kate's daydream ended when Dana dropped her laundry
basket on top of the article. A pretty young woman with long
blonde-streaked hair in a ponytail sauntered in and distracted

Kate. Her tight black jeans accentuated a well-toned body. Light makeup flattered her perfect features. Kate wondered if she was a model or a dancer. The girl hugged a dark-haired man who assisted her with her laundry. Kate's pain returned as her mood got darker.

Dana had her eyes on the same guy and purposely tipped the basket over, scattering her underwear and linens near his feet, hoping to cajole him away from the sexy *brasileira*. The hunk helped Dana retrieve her laundry and then turned his attention back to the girl.

Kate shook her head and whispered into Dana's ear, "Yo, you think he's Prince Charming? Why isn't he exchanging phone numbers with you? I remember him ogling her last Saturday at Key Food. He practically made love to her in the produce aisle. Dana, you're not his damsel in distress, and you don't know enough Portuguese to last the night!"

Dana replied, "I'll have to place another ad in *New York* magazine, or perhaps post one on the internet. Jesus, I think I'm already over the hill. The bar scene sucks! What the fuck am I supposed to do, Kate? I am still menstruating and could have children but, shit, I can't compete with the younger women. I hate doing laundry for one." She threw her gray towels back into the basket.

From the wash to the spin cycle, Kate told Dana about her recent nightmares, as the sexy girl pranced over to the dryers, removing expensive thongs and bras. Kate supposed that the girl's Ralph Lauren sheets could tell stories of lively romps with

Prince Charming and other royal studs. Hardly the stuff made from her own dreams.

Kate asked Dana if she still kept in touch with Sarah since she went MIA in answering her emails and phone calls.

Dana answered, "Not at all. Like with you, she never phoned or emailed." Dana changed the subject. "You know, Kate, we should adopt a kitten from a shelter. A kitty will give unrequited love without the bullshit, and unlike dogs, you don't have to walk them. Men are like dogs, always slobbering over you for sex and, boy, do they need to be trained. I've heard that female cats are easier to handle than male cats. They'll be spayed, so we don't have to listen them whine about not getting laid. We hear enough of that at work and at the bars. How 'bout it?"

After Kate pulled her bedspread out of the dryer and plunked it on the folding table, she replied, "A cat? Did our mothers have us altered when we were born and forget to tell us? Is the AARP rocking chair far behind? Why are you throwing in the towel at thirty-five?" She threw her towel at Dana.

Dana caught it, and Kate chuckled and said, "If a cat will keep us happy without a man to keep us warm, then let's go get ourselves a kitty—one for you and one for me."

Dana abandoned her clean laundry because Kate's magazine looked much more interesting. She skipped to the Restaurant section and drooled over Monsieur Paul. Kate swung her humongous canvas bag at her friend in jest and missed. The bag accidentally slapped the sexy girl's behind. Dana saw this and said *meow!* Kate apologized, while the hunk laughed at his girlfriend.

Kate and Dana sped up the folding. Dana, who understood the argument in Spanish and Portuguese, learned that the guy's name was José Maldonado, and he was, apparently, now available. She promised to reward Kate for her unexpected intervention by treating her tonight at the bistro.

*

Later that day, Kate and Dana took the F train to Bergen Street in nearby Cobble Hill. Dana, never too tired for conversation, rambled on about her premonition of meeting José Maldonado. She scanned the entrance to Bistro Saint Michel, and then it happened—he walked in. Dana introduced herself to José and invited him to sit next to her.

Given the way Dana touched his arm and held his hand, Kate was hesitant to trespass on her territory. And now that Dana had a date, Kate doubted that Dana would need a cat. Kate counted the minutes before her exclusion from the conversation. Being the designated third wheel tended to be her fate when others were coupled.

After tuna nicoise, grilled salmon, salad, bread, and a carafe of white wine, the crème brûlée arrived, accompanied by coffee, and later, the check. José insisted on paying for Dana and Kate, and handed his platinum American Express card to the waiter. He thanked the two women for the pleasant evening after the unfortunate encounter with his now ex-girlfriend, Cláudia, at the Laundromat earlier that day.

He gave Dana a continental peck on each cheek and cordially did the same with Kate. Kate pretended to be flattered. Dana exchanged phone numbers with him. Kate knew better than to do the same. She would probably have been just as possessive had the roles been reversed.

A gratified Dana hugged Kate. "I had a hunch he'd be here tonight. Now, what do we do about you?"

Kate's envious green eyes looked away, and she said, "I think a cat would do me fine, though I'm sure you don't need one now, sweetie."

It never took Dana long to cultivate a new relationship after a break-up. Kate, however, could no more remember the last time she had a date than she could remember the last time she had gone to confession.

They boarded the F train back to Seventh Avenue in Park Slope and strolled past the shops. Dana insisted on window shopping, until she screamed out, "Look, Kate. You will not spend your days alone much longer. Read this!"

She pointed to a handwritten sign announcing the sale of six three-month-old kittens at $25 each. "Kate, you must adopt! Jesus Christ, Sally, the cat lady, lives above you in Apartment 4B. I'm sure Anne won't mind a cat in the apartment; didn't you tell me she had one that died a few months ago? Let's drop by Sally's place. How convenient is that!"

Kate snarled, "What happened to *your* cat? Well, I assume things are different now."

98

Dana answered, "Oh, since José came into the picture? Let's be honest, Dana. I don't want a kitty to come between me and a potential spouse."

Dana hugged Kate and assured her that her turn would come; that Kate should adopt a kitty first, and everything else would fall into place.

*

The next morning, Kate rang Sally, the cat lady's, doorbell. Kate immediately fell in love with the only calico kitten amid Sally's litter of black and white and tortoiseshell kitties. Kate kissed the kitten's ginger and black spots. The room resonated with her purrs, and Kate noticed that the doll-like calico resembled Chloe, the stuffed animal in her childhood bedroom, which she used to hug during thunderstorms or after a bad day at school. The cute kitten came right up to Kate, bumped her head against her calves, and circulated her cat-like magic by rubbing her body around hers. She established her territory and now owned Kate, not vice versa, of course. Kate decided to call her *Amber,* and the kitty seemed to like it better than her original name, Ginger Snap. She paid Sally the $25 but had to leave the kitten there until she could purchase a litter box, a bed, food, and other feline essentials.

Kate released Amber, but the frisky kitten came back for more head-bumping and body-rubbing. She stood on her hind legs and placed her front paws on the bottom of Kate's denim skirt.

After the transaction, the women exchanged farewells. Tired from all the frolicking, Amber curled up in the corner, burying her face until she fell asleep. Sally closed the door as Kate walked downstairs.

Dana yelled "Congratulations" from the second-floor landing, and Kate accused her of being a snoop. Dana inquired whether the cat was female, and Kate answered *yes*. Dana asked the cat's name, when the animal was coming home, and if she could assist Kate with the shopping at Kitty Palace. Kate answered the rest of her questions, and they both agreed to meet the next day at eleven a.m. for pet store shopping.

After locking the door, Kate checked the vicinity, room by room, imagining where little Amber would sleep. She determined that the kitty should sleep in her new mommy's room and the litter box should be situated near the toilet. Kate reflected on her interview next Tuesday at Jennings, Holmes and Rogers Associates. *It will be nice to see Brent again*, she thought as she undressed, humming Natalie Cole's "Unforgettable." In the shower, she sang a Tom Jones tune from her childhood, "What's New Pussycat?" meowing after each *whoa*. The warm water soothed her as she blew bubbles with the suds.

*

The next morning, Dana helped Kate set up the cat items they'd purchased at Kitty Palace. Upon arriving in her new home, Amber backed away into a corner and watched. With the litter box filled, the cat bed set up, and some food and water placed in kitty dishes, Kate said *thank you* and *goodbye* to Dana.

Kate wanted to be alone to bond with Amber. But after Dana left, Amber quietly stayed in the corner.

"Come, Amber, don't be afraid," beckoned Kate. "Look, baby, see the mouse?" She shook the catnip mouse a few times. However, the calico seemed frightened in her new environment, and Kate told herself that she must be patient with her fur baby. She placed her in the litter box so that she could smell something familiar. Kate headed for the kitchen and brought the water tray and chicken-flavored cat food to the bathroom entrance, hoping that Amber would respond to the food.

Amber stepped backward as Kate moved the trays closer to the mewling kitten. Kate picked Amber up, trying to relax her, and gently rocked her back and forth as if she were a human baby. Amber did calm down, burying herself inside Kate's arms, refusing to leave her new refuge. Every time she put her down, the kitten whimpered. Kate's self-control crumbled. Desperate to feed her, she placed a treat in the kitten's mouth, and the kitten ate it. She tossed some catnip mice; however, Amber backed away and let out a cry, and then fled into the kitchen.

Kate lost her patience. Like a man, this kitty demanded too much attention. Amber refused to obey, which surprised Kate, since she thought female cats were supposed to be mellow.

"That's it, Missy, no food for you! You'd better behave, or else you'll have to eat your own shit. Now that wouldn't be too cool, would it?"

Not knowing what to do about the agitated cat, Kate called Dana on her cell phone. "Dana, Amber's wailing and refuses to eat unless I hand-feed her. I don't think she likes me. Listen to her! She whines and shakes like she's battery-operated."

Dana told Kate to relax, that the kitten might still be uncomfortable in her new surroundings and would eventually settle down. In the meantime, she suggested that Kate toss some catnip toys to pacify her. Although Kate did everything that Dana said, Amber did not let up, and finally, Dana told her to call Sally.

Out of pride, Kate refused, and hung up. There were caterwauls coming from the kitchen. After hearing several knocks on the door, she slid the peephole open and saw Dana and Sally together.

The door opened and Amber fled down the stairs and hid underneath the stairwell. The women called to her. Amber crawled to the darkest corner, pressing her body against the cool floor tiles. Kate and the others ran down the stairs, chanting *Amber, come here, baby.* Kate saw her tiny head peek out from behind the banister on the ground floor. She extended her hand, but Amber refused to budge. Kate waited for Sally to return with a towel, portable kitty carrier, and treat bag. She watched her place a treat before the kitten. Amber's right paw dragged it closer. She saw Kate and ran toward her and jumped into her arms. Amber purred and buried her head next to her breast, sniffing the warm jasmine and lily scent, and fell asleep.

102

Kate carried the cat back to the apartment, and Dana and Sally followed. Soon Amber woke up, stretching her pink mouth into a yawn. Kate placed her in the wicker kitty bed in her room, adjacent to her bed. She gave her a cat doll and Amber hugged it like a pillow.

"She's a little sensitive," whispered Sally. "Call me if you continue to have a problem. I understand how frustrating it can be with your first cat."

"Take it easy, Kate. I'll be here for you," Dana reassured her, as she patted her on the back.

Dana ordered a thin-crust pizza with peppers, pepperoni, and mushrooms for two from Pizza Al Horno. Amber joined them in the kitchen, drinking water and eating tuna.

Kate attached catnip toys to the scratching post in an effort to make it more inviting than tearing up the sofa nearby. She planned to trim the cat's claws in a few weeks—too painful to think about declawing. Sally said it was barbaric to maim a cat—*how would you like it if someone broke each of your fingers just because you have nails?*

The kitten sprang into her lap, distracting her owner with her cuteness. Kate pulled her lunch out of Amber's reach and shoved her away. The kitten slowly paced backward before pressing her bottom to the floor with her eyes still on the auburn-haired human, and left a smelly present.

Kate scolded the kitten. "You mischievous little brat! I'm the boss, not you. Do you pay rent here, kitty dear?"

Amber's sheepish expression dissolved Kate's annoyance. Reluctantly, Kate fed her a kitty treat and kissed her head. She cleaned up the mess and threw it in the litter box, trying to show Amber exactly where her feces ought to go. The kitty stepped into the sand this time, and Kate rewarded her with another treat.

Dana applauded. *"Brava,* Cat Woman. You've done it. Now you can get a life."

"Looks like I have a lot to learn about raising a kitten. Thanks again for helping me schlep the pet store purchases."

"Hey, Kate, I'll be around. Remember, you told me earlier today that you have an interview with handsome Brent MacDonald next Tuesday."

Beethoven's Fifth Symphony vibrated inside Dana's jeans pocket. José's cellular number popped up, and her tone sweetened. She told him to hold on, motioning to Kate that she had a date tonight and couldn't stay much longer. She kissed her cheek and waved goodbye to the cat.

Chapter 10

Kate
(2001)

Amber's energy amused Kate, as she watched the kitty leap from one end of the sofa to the other. The kitten knocked the lamp over. Fortunately, it landed on the sofa. Kate scolded her, remembering to use the proper vocal tone in order to demonstrate authority, as she had read in the kitty guidebook.

Kate stretched the kinks in her lower back, and said, "Kitty, dear, playtime is over for now. I'm going to prepare your dinner and mine."

With her pink-tinted ears pointed upward, the kitten jumped off the stool and followed her mistress. In the kitchen, Kate chopped up some veggies for a salad. Amber climbed up onto the counter and watched the knife dice the tomatoes and cucumbers. She drew nearer, placing her nose on the cutting board. Kate's swift reflexes stopped the knife in mid-air.

Sensing imminent danger, Amber backed away and jumped off the counter. She sat down by the refrigerator and groomed herself with her tongue. Kate finished her chopping, pleased and relieved. She hummed as she prepared the salad dressing. She had a feeling that Amber would sleep like an angel tonight.

As Kate was taking her shower after dinner and dishwashing, a feeling of discomfort overtook her. She had never owned a pet before and it felt odd to be *au naturel* with her new roommate. As a child, Kate could not have pets due to her father's allergies, and her previous landlords said no to pets too. She covered herself in a white terry robe and entered her dormlike bedroom, with the pitter-patter of little paws behind her. Amber stretched out on the throw rug in front of the twin bed. Kate walked to the other side for privacy, but the kitten was curious and wanted to see what her mistress would do next.

"Amber, leave me alone! Go over there! That's right, baby," demanded Kate, pointing to the cat bed.

Amber walked backward and bumped into the dresser. She wailed, licked her bottom, and rolled over onto the throw rug in an attempt to lure her mistress's attention. When Kate ignored her, the kitten growled. However, Kate refused to relinquish her authority. Amber gradually quieted down and crawled into her wicker kitty bed.

After putting on a baby tee and panties, Kate climbed into bed. The kitty was resting comfortably on her pink cushion in the kitty bed, but after a few minutes decided to wander to Kate's bed instead. The process repeated itself until Kate grabbed a treat and begged Amber to stay in her little nook. Kate flicked off the light on the nightstand, praying for peaceful sleep.

Amber missed the warmth of her human mother and crept under Kate's covers and began to knead the front of her shirt. She rubbed her mouth against one of her breasts. As she

106

proceeded to suck, Kate screamed at Amber to stop. The kitten darted out of Kate's bed after Kate threw a goose-down pillow at her a few times, missing on each attempt. Feathers flew, as did Kate's temper. Exasperated, she threatened to cast the cat out if she didn't behave. Once again, she directed Amber to the kitty bed. This time, she denied her the treats. The kitten crawled back to her sleeping quarters, lowered her head, and meowed pitifully. Kate buried her head under the pillows in order to drown out the whines. Several minutes passed before the kitten drifted into slumber, and shortly after, Kate did the same.

*

She entered the dreamscape again and found herself back in the dense woods. Everything looked the same—the gray-blue sky of twilight or dusk, the intense fragrance of exotic flora, and the tree near the bushes, forever on fire—forever crying in agony.

She saw the pond before her and gazed at her reflection. In that reflection, she saw the child, Allie, in her dated blue and white dress, standing beside her. Allie smiled as she carelessly held a shaky Amber. Amber's mouth was open, yet she didn't utter a sound. Allie roughly stroked the kitten's head. Kate ordered Allie to hand Amber back to her, but Allie refused. In a stern voice, Allie reprimanded Kate for the way she had handled the kitten at bedtime, and she wanted to know why Kate had stopped writing her story, warning her that both Kate and the kitten were now in grave danger.

107

"Kate, do you remember Sarah Kahn? She was in trouble until I helped her, and she, in return, helped me by writing my story. Why did you delete her from your life? She's a nice person, and you really should seek out her advice."

"You're full of shit!" shouted Kate. "I will write this story when I feel like writing it, without any help from you or Sarah, and I'm also taking back my cat." She grabbed the jittery feline from Allie.

Amber's teeth pierced Kate's left hand and she dropped the kitten. Amber fled to the adjacent bushes.

Kate's hand stung from the bite and blood seeped from the wound. She blew on it, applying pressure with her T-shirt to stop the bleeding, as Allie vehemently scolded her for hurting the cat.

Amber's shrieks ended abruptly and Kate feared that she was dead. The tree flared wildly and moaned as fresh blood dripped down its bark. The stone-faced Allie now accused Kate of murder, and Kate sobbed like a heartbroken child.

Amber's pink tongue awakened Kate from her dream, but Kate pushed her aside. Amber hissed in protest. A scratch burned Kate's left hand and bloodstains dotted her shirt. Kate assumed that the cat had scratched her while she was having that nightmare. She attributed Allie's shenanigans to her own stress and imagination. *Fuck this story*, she thought defiantly; she would stick to using her writing skills to make a living, even if it meant holding on to her shitty job at Focus NYC. *How the hell had Sarah come into the dream?* She decided it might be a good idea to call her. Kate had dumped Sarah's email address, but she thought she might have her phone number somewhere.

She placed Amber in her kitty bed before tending to her wound, thinking that perhaps it hadn't been so smart to adopt a cat. Kate decided, somewhat reluctantly, to return the cat to Sally after breakfast. She washed up, got dressed, and made breakfast. She turned on the radio to catch the news while she set up the kitty trays. She called for the kitty to come in, but there was no response.

Kate frantically checked each room, calling for Amber, but it seemed that the cat had disappeared again. She recalled her dream and panicked as she looked out the bedroom window, realizing that she had forgotten to close it last night. She ran out of the apartment, crying for help. A few neighbors came to her assistance. Dana heard the commotion and flew up the stairs, and Sally ran down, fearing the worst. Both women brought the distraught Kate back into the apartment. They rushed into Kate's bedroom, where cat urine reeked from the kitty bed.

Kate shivered as she gave the details of Amber's disappearance. She confessed that it was lack of patience or, rather, her bad dream, that probably sent Amber running. Dana and Sally calmed Kate down by assuring her that it was not her fault and that nightmares were just nightmares. They checked the area around the window, while some of the curious neighbors waited in the hallway, anxious to hear the latest developments. Dana suggested searching the bottom of the stairwell, since that was the place Amber had fled to the first time she ran away.

Dana hurried down the stairs and Kate followed her, calling Amber's name, but they could not find the cat.

Back in Kate's apartment, they checked the fire escape outside the open bedroom window and noticed a trail of blood leading to the backyard. The kitten had probably hurt herself by rubbing against the sharp nailhead, or maybe she was attacked by another cat.

One of the neighbors, Sushma Kumar, brought her nervous six-year-old son, Tommy, forward. The boy stammered, claiming to have seen a calico kitty from his window, going toward the bushes. They all headed to the entrance leading to the backyard. The boy followed the search party, which included several tenants. He directed them to where he had last seen the cat. The trail of blood on the fire escape and pavement led to the bushes. Kate called for Amber, until she caught a glimpse of fur hidden underneath the rhododendron bush. She pushed the branches aside, and what she saw shocked her.

Amber was alive, but she had lost an eye and her right ear. Portions of fur had been ripped off, and deep sores covered her left side, from her head down to her neck and across her body. She backed away from Kate skittishly.

Dana screamed, "Kate, what's wrong? Please tell me."

With all attention trained on Kate, Amber was given enough time to make her getaway through the alley. The driver of a furniture delivery truck passed through and didn't see the tiny cat dart in front of him. The wheels of his truck struck the animal, causing a *thump*. He heard a screeching sound underneath the vehicle and he stopped to take a look, shaking his head at his gruesome discovery. Kate wanted to lift the cat's mangled body and cradle her in her arms but couldn't. Instead, she threw up.

Using common sense with a gentle touch, Sally held her back and said, "Kate, please remember her as she was when you first saw her. Her spirit is at peace, and I know she loved you. You did your best."

Kate heard nothing, now realizing that the dream had been an omen. She blamed herself for Amber's cruel death, and wept, lamenting the fact that she had stopped writing *The Allie Chronicles*, now certain that there was a connection.

The truck driver apologized profusely as Sally carried the cat by her hind legs and placed her in a plastic bag. Then the truck driver departed and the crowd dispersed.

Dana escorted Kate upstairs and assisted her in removing the kitty bed and all the other cat-related items. When Kate burst into tears during the clean-up, Dana urged her to sit down and rest. She understood that her friend needed some time to mourn.

*

Deciding that her friend could use a little TLC, Dana put her romp with José on hold and stayed with Kate for the night. Kate had been on an emotional roller coaster with her job, sex life, and family, and now this. Dana finished cleaning up the mess at the window. Later, Caitlin Reilly, the landlady, brought up a tray of chocolate chip pecan cookies for Kate to share with Dana, and offered her condolences. She opined that a local tomcat might have mauled the kitty. She mentioned that little Tommy recalled Amber burying bits of her fur under the rhododendron bush. Other neighbors dropped by to offer their condolences, while others brought flowers. Tommy's mother, Sushma, delivered a pot of lamb biryani.

Dana asked Kate if she wanted Amber to be cremated and have her ashes placed in an urn for either a burial or to keep in her room. Kate said no, opting to have her buried, without the cremation, in the backyard.

They shared the meal and a bottle of red wine. For dessert, they ate the cookies and drank Earl Grey tea. The phone rang. It was Sally. Kate thanked her for her kindness but firmly stated that she didn't want to accept two kitties as a gift. In the mirror, she saw her own eyes narrow like a cat's, and she turned away.

Dana listened to Kate rant about how she hated it when people acted pushy and sweet at the same time, and reiterated her vow not to adopt any more cats, at least for now. Dana tried to console her and told her not to pay attention to Sally. She apologized to Kate for pressuring her into cat adoption. Besides, she said, "You need a man, not a cat." Dana immediately changed the subject to Kate's upcoming interview—*do you have your résumé ready and do you know what you'll be wearing?* Dana offered Kate another chewy cookie, figuring that a few extra bites would not cause any discernible weight gain.

Kate munched on a pecan chunk, yawning between each bite. She said, "I'm hitting the sack soon. Please turn off the light for me and leave the dishes in the sink. I'll do them tomorrow morning. I hope the sofa is comfortable. Have a nice rest, Dana, and thanks for your help."

"No! You're the one who needs the rest," answered Dana. "I don't mind taking care of the dishes."

Dana kissed her on the head and carried the cups and saucers on the serving tray to the kitchen. Dana forgot to turn off the light, and Kate got up to do it herself, and then climbed back into bed.

*

Kate fell asleep and found herself back in the forest. She heard Amber wailing. The raggedy kitty looked the way she had when Kate last saw her in the gutter. As Kate got closer, Amber transformed into her stuffed cat, Chloe. The toy hung over a crude device made of wood above an untended campfire and sang a sad melody. Like a piece of meat, a sharp branch with two sticks supporting it speared the toy from its mouth to its rear end. Tiny sparks shot upward, licking the toy's partially skinned body, and the song faded into the crackling flames. Like a giant teardrop, the cat's one good eye dropped from its socket. The angry flames devoured Chloe, leaving ash and charred materials to smolder. A scent reminiscent of barbecued meat lingered as the campfire weakened and died. In the background, she heard an explosion, and then another. Moaning and shedding more blood, the tree burned in torment.

Dana heard Kate sighing and woke her up, understanding that Kate's grief had no place to go and that even sleep offered her no solace. Dana listened as Kate recounted the details of the dream, and offered words of comfort and a cup of chamomile tea.

Dana turned off the light and kept the door ajar. Oddly, she saw an apparition by the window. Kate noted a smile on her friend's face and asked what happened. Dana pointed to the window—however, the image disappeared before Kate could turn her head.

"Sweetie, I saw Amber by the window," said Dana. "She looked adorable and happy. I'm sorry you missed it. Now get some rest! You have a big week ahead." She flicked off the light and shut the door.

Alone, Kate wondered if her baby forgave her. She had missed Amber's apparition, but it only would have upset her. Was Dana imagining this? Were dreams a way for the mind to become cognizant of what would happen? Was Amber's death a coincidence? *Maybe not,* she thought. Did she dream of Chloe as a substitute for Amber? Were Chloe and Amber merely symbols for unattainable love? Was Kate the burning tree that bled and cried for help—the forest, her life—the creature, her fear of men, and Allie, her spirit guide? *Maybe yes,* she thought.

Chapter 11

Kate
(2001)

On Sunday night, Kate rummaged through her closet for the perfect interview outfit. She wasn't sure whether she should wear the charcoal gray Theory suit or the black Tahari. Both suits required ironing. A white cotton shirt would do, but her black Charles Jourdan pumps required extra polish. Kate treated her interview like a date, but since it wasn't until Tuesday, she could attend to these matters on Monday evening. She closed the closet door and retired to a night of browsing through *Vogue* for fashion tips and *The New Yorker* for articles of interest. The weather forecast on TV was predicting bad weather for Tuesday due to Hurricane Erin. The forecast depressed Kate, whose mind wandered back to her dead cat, the disfigured man, the precocious Allie, and her stuffed animal, Chloe. She forced herself to concentrate on the magazines.

A co-worker at Estée Lauder had once hinted that she needed to do something about her appearance, because doors never budged for ordinary girls unless Daddy or Mommy were related to the company chiefs or had inflated bank accounts. She took advice from *Cosmopolitan, Allure,* and *Vogue.* She had laser surgery and threw away her glasses. Trips to makeup counters became her single woman's version of the Magic

Kingdom. She opened up charge accounts and never left home without her American Express card. She emerged out of her shell to be promoted to associate copywriter. She started dating, although never seriously enough to go from point A, as in *attraction,* to point B, as in *bed.* A few rotten dates groped her in the 'A' stage, leaving her feeling humiliated and disrespected. But she didn't want to give up on men entirely, and she had to admit, thinking of Brent was starting to excite her.

Kate browsed through her magazines. In *The New Yorker,* she read an article on the West Coast poet Margaret Altman. Kate used to write poetry and had attended open mics in the Village and TriBeCa while a student at NYU. There was something about Ms. Altman's physical features that reminded her of Sarah Kahn. She read her two poems, "Lost" and "The Life That Wasn't." Inspired by the poet's simplicity, Kate felt a desire to write poetry again, and wondered if she had wasted her time and energy on *The Allie Chronicles.* Perhaps she could take what she had written and repurpose it for her poems.

Seeing Sarah in the poet's face, Kate decided she would contact her ex-roommate next week. She convinced herself that a reunion would be nice, and doubted that Dana would mind. She flipped off the light and had a restful seven hours of sleep.

Chapter 12

Kate
(2001)

A gentle breeze filtered past the aluminum vent as sunshine filtered through the blinds. Hurricane Erin had decided not to visit the Big Apple after all. Although theoretically summer, fall had arrived unexpectedly this Tuesday morning.

Kate woke up before the 6:45 alarm. Like thousands of women in the business world, she set herself on a routine of a morning shower and cosmetic application, but today she went one step further—she wanted to please Brent.

She decided to wear the charcoal gray Theory suit. The cut emphasized her trim waist, while streamlining the rest of her figure. The deep copper water-based hair dye complemented her pale complexion.

The outfit came together in less than ten minutes. Her pink pearl earrings and colorful Hermès scarf would offset her monochromatic look. She slipped into her black Charles Jourdan pumps, slung her black Chanel strap bag over her shoulder, and grabbed her Louis Vuitton valise, which was armed with her résumé and cover letter. She took one last look in the mirror to bolster her confidence, and gave herself final approval before dashing out. Kate reminded herself to leave by 9:15 in order to have ample time for transportation. She had lied to Jackie about a doctor's appointment at ten.

Just as she swiped her MetroCard, the R train rolled in at Union Street Station. Miraculously, she got a seat. Once in the City, Kate dropped by Java Muffin for her usual coffee and blueberry crumb muffin, and she and her breakfast got to her desk by 8:27. Before settling into her chair, she noticed the light for voicemails. Brent had left a message, asking her to call him as soon as she arrived. With her heart palpitating, she dialed, and after two rings the efficient Christy Sinclair answered, with a tone of plastic perkiness befitting an executive secretary. Kate identified herself and asked to speak with Mr. MacDonald, reminding Madame Christy about her scheduled interview with him today at ten. Ms. Sinclair put Kate on hold. During the Muzak interlude, Kate imagined that the bitch probably had Brent as her security blanket, and Kate wanted to rip it from her hands. A minute later, Ms. Sinclair's chirpy voice returned and connected Kate to Brent.

"Hi, Kate, how are you?" said Brent. "I'm sorry to cancel on such short notice, but I have an emergency meeting at ten."

Kate's enthusiasm plummeted. Sick of her programmed etiquette, her hand tightened on the receiver, wondering what else could go wrong.

"Let me check my planner, Kate. Umm, I'm free today at three. Are you available then, or would you prefer to reschedule for Friday at ten?"

"I can come in at three today," answered Kate. Her desperation increased, as she thought of how much she wanted Brent and the perks of a higher-paying position—having her own apartment, taking trips to Europe, buying more clothes, and pampering herself, without the worries of day-to-day survival. She could tell her boss that the doctor had been called to an emergency and had to switch her appointment time.

"Kate, can you repeat what you said? There's a rumbling noise outside."

She raised her voice, but his voice went in and out. "I can't hear you either. Brent, Brent, Brent, can you hear me? Sounds like a bad connection. Brent?"

Brent couldn't answer Kate. After turning his swivel chair toward the windows, the glass crashed. Flames jumped forward. Office furniture, lamps, plants, files, computers, papers, pens, and pencils either flew out the windows or toward the inferno. The conflagration spared nothing in its path. Degrees and awards from Harvard, plaques from the Ad Council and Focus NYC, photos taken with Mayor Giuliani and President Bush, prints by Paul Klee, and some rare wooden Chinese artifacts from the 16th century crumbled into cinders. Brent's body turned to ash as the destruction began.

*

Kate held on to the receiver, baffled by the abrupt disconnection. As Kate hung up, Ellen Price, another fashion writer, came bounding over to her desk.

119

"Kate, did you hear the news? A plane just hit the North Tower of the World Trade Center. Probably a new pilot learning to fly a small plane. Not a lot of details yet, so I don't know if anything serious happened."

Kate didn't answer. Her hand knocked over her coffee, and hot liquid spilled on her desk, her skirt, and the floor.

"Oh, Kate, I hope you didn't burn yourself. Let me help you clean it up. Use some cold water or club soda on it immediately. I don't think this will stain your nice suit. Lucky for you, you're wearing a dark color."

Observing Kate's vacant face, Ellen asked, "Are you okay? You look pale. Would you like a cup of tea from the kitchen? I'll fetch some paper towels and club soda." Kate nodded, and Ellen patted her on the arm.

Ellen returned with a Styrofoam cup of piping hot tea with sugar, a bottle of club soda, and paper towels. Intense heat rose from the cup as she glanced at the CNN news coverage in the video conference room. Enormous gray and white clouds poured out of the steel girder skin of the North Tower. Tea spilled on her hand as she hurried back to Kate's cubicle.

Ellen poured the club soda on the towel and rubbed it on Kate's skirt, repeating the process until the only evidence of the stain was a dark wet circle.

"Let it dry and it'll be fine," said Ellen.

Kate nodded again, drank the tea, and cleaned the mess on her desk, while her colleague wiped the spill off the industrial

120

gray carpet. Voices filled the hallway, and Ellen peeked outside. More employees headed toward the video conference room.

Ellen said, "I'm going to check out the latest news. Do you want to come?"

Kate put down her cup and followed her in the mass exodus down the hall. Several people sat in front of the thirty-inch TV screen. Ellen sat next to Kate. Others drifted in one by one, until it was standing room only. Buzzing questions of *why* and *what do we do now* bounced back and forth. The oddly calm atmosphere felt like being in the eye of a hurricane.

The story worsened. Another plane hit the South Tower, and there was a confusing account of a third plane hurtling into the Pentagon. Kate watched in disbelief. Her questions juxtaposed without answers as both towers burned like giant candlesticks against the brilliant September sky. Reports drifted in. All the planes were reported as hijacked, and all aboard were either dead or missing. Kate's mind blocked the numbers when the figures became too jarring.

Everyone waited for direction from the White House, Gracie Mansion, and the CEO of Focus NYC. All airports had closed. The Port Authority of New York and New Jersey had closed down the bridges and tunnels, and the subways had shut down. Cell phones lost signals. Kate learned that Manhattan was an island cut off from its neighbors. Like everyone else, she wanted to go home.

The CEO, Mark Bernstein, stepped up to the podium. He announced that the workday was over but urged everyone to remain calm and wait a few hours until the human traffic over the bridges and streets lessened. Regarding whether there would be work the following day, Mr. Bernstein suggested that employees call the company's emergency number in the morning.

Kate and several co-workers wanted to leave immediately, understandably nervous about getting home. They watched in shock as the South Tower fell like a house of cards. Kate listened quietly to the outbursts—a few cried—a few had relatives and friends who worked at the Twin Towers—a few wanted to wage war on terrorists—a few complained about the government.

The CEO reassured everyone that President Bush was doing everything possible to protect America. Susan Rhodes, one of the Human Resources representatives, stood by the CEO's side. She presented a short speech on the company's concern for its employees and for those who had loved ones trapped at the World Trade Center. She gave a phone number for those who wished to seek professional help. After the pep talk, both Mr. Bernstein and Ms. Rhodes disappeared into their offices.

Kate didn't want to return to her cubbyhole. She saw co-workers leaving, with or without consent. She wanted to go to Astoria, where her father lived. If her father wasn't home, she could stay at Ellen's on the other side of Steinway Street.

Kate dialed her father. "Dad, it's me, Katie. I'm waiting to be released from work, perhaps in an hour or two. I need to ask you a favor. I'd like to stay over in my old room. It's too far to walk to Brooklyn. The world is going to hell. I'm scared, Dad. I don't know if my future boss is dead or alive. I was supposed to be interviewed by him today for a copy position. I hope he was able to escape to the roof for a helicopter rescue." She paused for a minute, and replied, "Okay, Dad, see you later."

Once off the phone, Kate motioned to Ellen. "Let's tell Jackie that we're going home to our families. Are you in?"

Ellen agreed, hoping the boss would be sympathetic and let her staff go home. They passed by the video conference room. A weird hush hovered over the room. The North Tower had collapsed. Although it had been hit first, the solo tower had enough resilience to outlast the South Tower. But not by much.

Horrified, Kate saw that not one helicopter came to rescue Brent or the other people on the upper floors. The City did nothing and allowed them to die. She imagined Brent's blue eyes and model-perfect smile fading into the flames. He must be dead! How could he have escaped when his office was on the ninety-ninth floor? Why was he in his office at the time she called? He should have left the building for breakfast or a workout—if he had, he would be alive now. *Damn you, Allie, and your machinations.* Screaming, she faced the wall and banged her fists in successive rhythm.

Ellen pulled her away and whispered, "Don't panic! It's going to be okay. Please be calm, it's going to be okay. Kate? Can you hear me, Kate?"

Although she received a mini-lecture from Anne Barrows on being strong and a complaint from Derek MacFallen on her self-pity, Kate heard nothing, because Brent was as dead as the future of the world. She'd had a taste of trouble in recent weeks. She couldn't cry because her tear ducts were still dry, especially when the ascending tension surmounted compassion. Ellen admonished the two co-workers for their lack of sensitivity toward her friend. They apologized, and both Ellen and Kate calmed down.

Ellen tapped Kate's hand. "I think it's time for us to go home. I'll walk you to your dad's house. Let's go to Her Highness and plead your case. Maybe there's an ounce of goodness in that wretched heart."

She escorted Kate to Jackie's office. The boss was on a personal call with her boyfriend but motioned for the women to come in. Ellen did all the talking, knowing that Kate was not particularly in good standing with the boss, recalling the problem Kate had had with the Summer Dress campaign. Kate's writing skills were apparently not innovative enough for Jackie, and Jackie and the vendors had demanded several rewrites.

Behind the red-rimmed frames, Jackie's eyes scrutinized Kate, and Kate suspected that Allie had been working her vengeance through her boss. Her tears finally released.

Jackie said, "Kate, I understand that you are upset, but we have to be strong for our nation during this crisis."

Ellen interrupted. "Jackie, don't you think it makes sense for some people to leave? Other divisions are allowing their employees to go home. I live near Kate and can escort her home."

"Ellen, I am following the company's protocol for you, Kate, and my other writers. As Mr. Bernstein said, it's best to wait it out. Right now, the Queensboro Bridge is probably jammed with people pushing and shoving. I think it would be wise to wait a few extra hours to ensure a safe journey home. I'm not trying to sound like the bad guy, but come on, Ellen, *think.*"

While the debate continued, Mike Shapiro, the Senior VP of Advertising and Marketing, knocked on the open door to announce that Mr. Bernstein had officially closed the office, and that everyone should go home. The office would be closed tomorrow, since Mayor Giuliani advised all employees in non-emergency jobs to take tomorrow off to reflect or be with their loved ones.

Ellen whispered in Kate's ear, "Girl, it's time to go."

As they left, Mike patted Kate's arm, and said, "Get home safe, and don't worry, there's no shame in having a good cry."

Chapter 13

Kate
(2001)

Walking along Second Avenue reminded Kate of a crowded street fair on a balmy day; however, this was no street fair. No vendors peddled kebabs, Italian ices, affordable fashions, or trinkets. No club music blared from booths—only a palpable sense of anxiety.

Kate walked side by side with Ellen. They had said little since leaving the office at 2:30. The traffic along Third Avenue moved at a pedestrian pace, and the Queensboro Bridge lay ahead. Before crossing the bridge, Ellen stopped by a deli for bottled water and granola bars. Ellen cautioned Kate that dehydration might be a problem, especially with the fumes traveling uptown, and that the sugar and protein boost from the power bars should energize them for their long journey to Queens.

At 59th Street, cops directed the crowd to stay to the right for vehicles to pass over the bridge. Crowds swelled in the designated walkways. Kate's stomach felt queasy and the strong sunlight gave her a headache. Her sloppy loafers comforted her feet, but her pumps added extra weight in her tote.

To her right, smoke-filled clouds hovered over Lower Manhattan. Overhead, a passing plane stirred a mild panic on the

126

bridge. Although a lapsed Catholic, Kate prayed for the ominous sound to go away.

Her friend read her face and hugged her. "Kate, it's all right. It's probably the armed forces patrolling the area. It would have been nice if we were alerted, but then again, we're not in front of a TV."

The walkways filled up like the subway during rush hour. Several people climbed over cement partitions and hopped into small trucks and vans, while other riders pulled some of them in.

Kate finally spoke. "It's the end of the world. Look at them, scrambling like mice. See that grinning jerk climbing onto that old pickup truck while smoke still rises over the East River? Maybe we should have waited till later. I'm tired and my feet are killing me." The leather on the old loafers had tightened around her swollen toes.

"Kate, I don't think it would have been wise to cross this bridge in the dark. The mob seems fairly civil. Besides, we're almost halfway across. Take a few gulps of water from this bottle. And here's a granola bar." Kate thanked her and broke off a piece of the bar and twisted the cap off the water bottle.

While wiping the residue moisture from her lips, she thought she heard a child calling her name. Kate dropped her tote and shoved her way through the crowd. Ellen grabbed Kate's tote and hollered for her to come back.

Kate slowed down and walked to the edge of the bridge. She found it hard to catch her breath and she leaned against a

127

steel pillar for support. She saw Ellen making her way through the mostly sympathetic crowd.

"Are you okay?" questioned Ellen. "We're halfway there, and when we get off this bridge, I think we should stop by a diner for something to eat and drink."

"Someone is following me," answered Kate. "A kid wearing a light blue and white dress was calling my name."

"What child? I was right by you and didn't hear anything. Now just take a few minutes to relax. Breathe in and out to the count of three."

Kate lost sight of Allie, but Ellen did see a child—a boy in red overalls and a yellow-striped shirt, walking beside his mother.

The boy, probably no more than six, tightened his hand in his mother's hand and cried, "When are we going to be home? I'm tired and hungry, Mommy." He yanked his mother's hand but failed to get her attention.

*

Ellen and Kate reached Long Island City and walked to Northern Boulevard under the N train's elevated tracks. They followed the bus route and turned left at the intersection to Steinway Street, and walked until they reached the Modern Age Diner.

At the diner, they found a vacant booth by the window. Kate sat down first and kicked off her shoes. A matron who looked to be in her mid-fifties welcomed them with a smile and

128

two menus. She brought two glasses of water and set them on the table.

Kate finally settled on the Santorini Chicken, served on a bed of orzo and tomato sauce, smothered in feta cheese, and a glass of Merlot. Ellen ordered the turkey club sandwich sans mayo and decided on a glass of Merlot rather than a Diet Coke. With her pencil ready, the waitress pulled out her pad, took their orders, and kept the conversation brief.

Kate checked her watch and realized she had forgotten to alert Dana that she wasn't coming home tonight. Kate didn't own a cell phone and hated to use public phones because of germs and *God knows what.*

"Kate, you could call her from your dad's," said Ellen. "Sorry I don't own a cell phone yet. Maybe she's stuck and plans to sleep over in the City? Do you have your landlord's number in your Filofax? I'm sure the building people will look after your apartment until you return tomorrow. Hopefully, the buses and subways will be back in service by then."

Kate's mind traveled elsewhere and she mumbled Brent's name. Tears trickled down her cheeks. She momentarily forgot that she was sitting across from Ellen.

The waitress brought the wine glasses on a tray, placed them by Ellen, and handed several napkins to Kate. Ellen offered the wine to her friend. Kate took a few sips of the average-quality wine and tore off a piece of Italian bread, spreading it with a thick coating of sweet butter. The piping hot chicken dish sat before her. Its aroma was tempting, but after a few minutes

129

she pushed it away and offered it to Ellen. When the bill came, Ellen snatched it and put it on her Visa card, while Kate protested.

The waitress thanked them and hugged them as they left. The two women continued their journey up Steinway Street and turned left on Broadway. A group of schoolchildren on the corner waved American flags, shouting, "If you believe in America, honk your horn!" They blew whistles to stop traffic. Like caped crusaders, the patriotic teenagers wore American flags. Ellen and Kate also wanted a piece of the red, white, and blue.

*

The next morning, Kate had a calm train ride back to Brooklyn. At nine a.m., the car was only half full. Several straphangers wore tri-colored ribbons, while others wore "I Love NY" T-shirts. Courtesy and kindness became the new norm. Kate's MetroCard had insufficient fare, but a man permitted her to use his card. The stations fast-forwarded—*next stop, Atlantic Avenue–Pacific Street.* Soon, Kate would be home.

She thought about Anne returning from Italy on Saturday to a jammed airport with heightened security measures. What a letdown it would be after sipping cappuccino at a café in a piazza and taking in all the sights of a living museum. Even more concerning, she wondered whether her roommate had any relatives or friends who had been trapped at the World Trade Center.

130

When she got to her stop, she headed to the stairwell and the sunshine on Fourth Avenue in Park Slope. The neighborhood felt strange as she walked up Ninth Avenue, as if this were her first visit to Brooklyn. She heard a cat wailing and thought of Amber. She sensed that the kitten still loved her—or did she? The noise persisted for a few minutes and then vanished. Kate continued eastward. She had left Astoria without eating and now her stomach craved coffee and a pastry. Regrettably, The Cookies & Creamery was closed. Upon arriving at her stoop, she saw the weathered calligraphy above the doorway and crossed the marble threshold, a stranger in her own building.

Kate's father had treated her like a stranger too. She couldn't stand being in his house one more day, and wished that her mother were still around, but her mother had succumbed to cardiac arrest five years ago. Too many memories of her father's authoritarian rule—his deprecating disapproval and his use of the strap. Although she planned to do volunteer work, he berated her for being selfish. According to him, all she thought about was travel, booze, and whining about men and work. She thought that her old man would soften in the wake of this crisis, but he hadn't.

As she walked up the stairs, each step applied more pressure to her legs. Her mood stiffened along with her calves, adding more weight to her ordeal. Apartment 3B came into view, with two attached yellow sticky notes from Dana on the door telling Kate that Dana had come back early this morning after staying over at her friend Gina's in Greenwich Village but left

131

early to visit her cousin Linda in Norwalk, Connecticut. The note included an invite to a weekend trip on Friday to Newport, Rhode Island.

Kate pulled the note off. She thought about her budget and whether this trip was doable.

Once in the apartment, the phone rang. It was Dana. "Hi, hon. Jesus Christ, what a goddamn mess we're in. The fucking world's exploding with terrorists and oilmen. Hey, before we drop dead, let's eat, drink, and be merry in style up in Newport."

"Dana, I can't just pack up and leave. I don't want Anne to come home to an empty apartment on Saturday."

Dana yelled, "She's a big girl and can handle the place for a few days without you. She left you alone for two weeks, and you're not allowed to take two-and-a-half measly days? Come on, Kate, get a life! Leave a note saying that you'll be with me up in Newport for the weekend for mental health recovery. I'll make arrangements for us to stay at a quaint B&B. Sharing a king-sized bed will save us some money. I'm sure there'll be vacancies, since it's after Labor Day."

Kate learned that Dana had recently dumped José. Dana, a *nice Jewish girl* whose gene pool could fill the United Nations, was at least an equal-opportunity offender, since all men were schmucks in any nationality. Dana insisted that this would be a girls' outing only, because girls needed schmucks with money and heart, not empty pockets and bullshit.

"Listen to the gold digger with balls," giggled Kate.

"Hey, don't knock me," laughed Dana. "At least I got you to laugh again. Now move your ass and find some cute outfits in your closet or buy new ones. I'll call you to let you know what time I'll be picking you up in Norwalk."

After hanging up the phone, Kate turned on the TV and heard more disturbing reports—the number of dead and missing had escalated, and the channels kept replaying the horror of the planes colliding into the towers, the explosion, and the collapse. The repeated video loops upset her, and the media made sure that she wouldn't ever forget.

After half an hour, she shut off the TV and turned on the radio. Radio station Z-100 had lost its humor to the 9/11 tragedy. Enrique Iglesia's song "Hero" catapulted him to the top of the charts, while Mariah Carey's own "Hero" hit made a comeback. The songs now contained superimposed news reports, adding another level of emotional impact.

The songs depressed her. Brent had died and she was still alive. He'd had everything going for him, while she didn't have much. Had Brent lived, would he have been interested in her? She never could keep a boyfriend—they stood her up, dumped her, or mistreated her. Yet she was planning to spend money just to make a fool of herself again. For some reason, this made her eager to get in touch with Sarah.

Kate checked her Rolodex for Sarah's number and dialed, but a recorded message stated that she was on vacation and wouldn't be back until next Saturday. Kate hung up without leaving a message. She would call Sarah next Sunday.

Meanwhile, Newport sounded great—the mansions along Bellevue Avenue, the boats, the seafood, and the tranquility of a New England town miles away from Ground Zero and those damn Allie dreams. The thought of this comforted her.

*

On Friday morning, Kate's alarm failed to go off at seven, the N train came late, and in the lobby of her office building, a security guard accosted her. "Miss, please open your suitcase and bag!"

Although Kate's photo ID matched her face, in this post–9/11 world, she was a potential terrorist. Her wet umbrella, hair, and jeans dripped puddles on the marble floor. Her life collided with New York City's climate and universal sadness.

Kate wished that the rain had waited until after she entered the building. A barrage of questions attacked her mind—*why was the rain coming down in buckets—why did this happen on the day she was leaving early for Newport—why did she have to prove that she wasn't carrying a bomb—why hadn't her alarm clock gone off at seven—why didn't the train come on time?*

She bit her lip and opened her wet handbag first. The nervous guard tried to impress her superiors, who were as nervous as she was. Her voice sounded more strident than authoritative. She made a swift examination of Kate's handbag and asked her to open up the suitcase. Kate complied, fumbling through her bag past a clutter of pens, tissues, mints, Filofax, cosmetics, purse, and papers before finding her luggage key. She bent down to unlock it. The guard now insisted that Kate open each plastic bag in order to expose the contents. Exasperated, she had no choice but to obey. Her neatly packed toiletries and clothes, now a jumbled mess, passed the safety test, and the guard thanked her for her cooperation.

No longer deemed a threat, Kate hurried to the elevators. She would tidy up her belongings once she settled down. She could use her Conair travel hairdryer to dry her jeans and hair. One of the six elevators waited for her and went express to the fifth floor.

The air conditioner at Focus NYC blasted arctic air on even the coolest and rainiest of days, and today was no exception. She couldn't complain that much on dress-down Friday, because for the long drive to Newport, jeans made the best attire. She rushed to her cubbyhole and connected the dryer. The inclement weather and security searches had delayed others as well, making Kate look punctual at 9:11. Everyone was looking for a temporary escape from New York this weekend.

After getting dry and putting her suitcase back in order, Kate settled into her workday. The jewelry insert for the November issue sat on her chair. Attached to its plastic folder was a nasty note scribbled in red—*Finesse hated the artwork and copy—a bolder approach needed with both. The vendor must see the corrected job ASAP.* The note went on to attack her competence as a writer. Anger pulsated throughout each letter, as if the pen had deliberately been dipped in blood. She imagined Jackie's trademark blood-red nails applying pressure to her felt-tipped pen, Jackie's vicarious thrill of stabbing her hapless writer. Because the client wasn't satisfied, Kate had to take the blame—a real class act, especially during this trying time. She tossed the job on her desk. Deadlines and bosses didn't give a shit if a Black Hole loomed on the horizon.

She opened the *Finesse* electronic folder and clicked on the Quark document. She typed several headlines: *A Scarf to Tie Around Your Neck—A Scarf to Wrap Around Your Neck—A Scarf to Wear Around Your Neck*. Her fingers aligned with neither her thoughts nor the keyboard. Her first three attempts were decidedly lackluster, but she tried again: *A Scarf to Tie For—Tie Dye Neck Lace*. The last two headlines played on the word *die—tie* for *die* and *dye* for *die*. How could she write about death when hundreds of people were either deceased or missing? The image on the screen showed a sophisticated brunette wearing a silk scarf splashed in watercolors—russet rose, amber gold, and sepia wood, under an outline of lace in brown ink, as described on the copy turn-in sheet. She reread it yet couldn't write a sales pitch without running into another snag. The model's swan-like neck inspired her to write *Swan Song,* but that too had an association with death. She struck out again, and death had been in the air since Amber's passing. She tried to write copy, not *The Allie Chronicles*, and panicked, thinking that Allie's curse was getting deeper. *What a shame Sarah is away. I could have questioned her about the dreams.*

Ellen came by and hugged her. "Dear Kate, please try to control yourself. This place should be classified as a war zone.

136

They seem to be sympathetic, but the powers that be will use this as evidence against you, no matter what they say about post–traumatic stress disorder. Be careful, since you are on Jackie's shit list! Hey, we have to think of those who perished and carry on in their memory. Do it for Brent! Giving money would be cool and donating a personal touch would be even more special. Maybe you and I can donate our time at Nino's."

"Let me wrap up this job first before I say yes," said Kate.

Ellen read the copy on the screen and exclaimed, "Why not use part of what you just said? *Wrap Up*. What a brilliant headline. Short, sweet, and punchy. An eye-catcher, like that sexy scarf."

Kate answered, "I was striking out all my ideas—too boring or too moribund or—like what's on my screen, *Swan Song.*"

Ellen read the yellow sticky note and sighed. "She's on a mission to get your ass. This vendor is being difficult. They want a bolder look on the model, which now requires a re-shoot, and the headline and copy to reflect this. From what I see, they are going after a younger audience." She dug into the folder and read the copy turn-in sheet. She shook her head and said, "The sheet clearly stated a sophisticated, mature, and upscale approach in art and copy. Your headline, *Status Symbols,* said this, and your copy supported it. Apparently, someone at *Finesse* changed their mind, and Jackie blamed you for it. I can almost see flames spitting out from the ink. God, I hope she doesn't shred your ad."

137

Kate typed in another headline, *Wrap City*. Both writers agreed that this would appeal to the younger Gen-Xers. Kate gazed again at the screen, thinking that her days at Focus NYC were growing shorter, like the season. She would have to get away from Jackie ASAP, before Human Resources threw her out. She thought of taking the silk scarf off the model's neck and tying it around her own. But she had to do her work, because no one wanted a curmudgeon around to disturb the equilibrium of office life.

Ellen saw the open suitcase and said, "Kate, does Jackie know you're taking off to Rhode Island?"

"Yeah," she responded. Ellen's banter was annoying her. "I told her yesterday, and she didn't say *boo*. Ellen, I need to finish these projects on my chair before I leave at three." She turned her back and hit the keyboard.

*

By eleven, a mellower Jackie approved the copy, and by noon, Jackie came over to say goodbye before leaving for Boston. She was going to visit her family and would not return until Tuesday. She preferred driving instead of dealing with airport security. She even wished Kate a safe and happy trip.

Ten minutes later, Ellen dropped by Kate's desk and told her to leave, since Jackie had fled the premises; they could finish their work on Monday. Kate waved her hand *no*. She wanted to finish these projects now, and didn't think it would take that long; by three, the latest. Before taking off, Ellen hugged Kate and wished her a safe trip to Newport.

By 3:15, Kate completed her tasks. Under normal circumstances, the four ads wouldn't have been arduous, even with the stringent requests from the vendors and from Jackie, but Kate's lack of concentration detained her. She should have listened to Ellen and left them for Monday, but her stubbornness compelled her to finish them.

She forgot about meeting Dana in East Norwalk by three.

Dana called and said she got worried when the 2:04 train pulled in and Kate wasn't on it. Kate apologized for her tardiness and promised to arrive by 5:30.

Kate suddenly felt a pang of envy that Dana had the good fortune to open her own clothes boutique in Brooklyn Heights, the upscale neighborhood where Dana's parents resided. Strange how that Ouija board had hit it on the nose when it predicted Dana's success. She knew that Dana had asked her assistant, Michelle Eisen, to handle the shop while she was away. Dana didn't have to report to anyone except herself. *No wonder she has that damn cheery attitude,* thought Kate.

She shut down her computer, turned off the lamp, and closed her repacked suitcase. She decided not to lock it, just in case she was selected for a random search at Grand Central. She wished her few remaining co-workers a nice weekend and rushed off to the elevators.

Her mood brightened as the elevator descended. When she rolled her suitcase past security, the guard who had searched her in the morning wished her a pleasant weekend, and Kate wished her the same. As she exited through the revolving doors, the warmth of the afternoon sun greeted her. Kate headed toward Park Avenue and walked south to Grand Central Station, smiling.

Chapter 14

Kate
(2001)

At Grand Central Station, the National Guard's presence was everywhere, but neither Kate nor her luggage got searched. She, like the other commuters, went about their business of purchasing tickets and waiting for their trains. Kate bought a one-way ticket for the New Haven-bound Metro-North train to East Norwalk, Connecticut. She had just missed the 4:02 by a few minutes. She wheeled her luggage amid the rush-hour herd to the gate for the 4:11 train. By the time she got on, only a few seats remained, and she had no choice but to sit next to a heavy-set man. Kate squirmed as her large seatmate spread into her territory. She wanted to place her suitcase on one of the racks, but all of them were taken—first come, first served—the survival of the earliest. She wished she had left with Ellen and avoided this rush-hour chaos. Her medium-sized luggage pressed against her legs and knees. Her jeans provided a buffer against the suitcase's rough canvas edges. Her neighbor kept spreading his legs, looking comfortable as he read his newspaper, while she moved further to the right with half her derriere hanging off the edge of the seat.

The train passed 125th Street and the green patches of the Bronx. According to the forecast, the weekend would be rain-free and summer would be sticking around for the next few weeks. On the surface, life seemed copacetic, but she felt cramped in her seat and PMS was causing a headache to circulate between her brows. With her holiday off to a shaky start, she bitched to herself that Dana could have made it more convenient by picking her up in Park Slope.

The train pulled into East Norwalk before 5:30. Kate dragged herself off the train, and her headache followed her. She trudged to the exit and stairs. Every step added weight to her luggage, and she felt just as heavy. By the last step, she almost collapsed.

A car turned on the corner of Washington Street and honked. Dana waved to her from the open window and yelled, "Jesus, you look like you've been through shit and back. You can tell me all the details later. For now, just get in and chill out. I'll put your luggage in the trunk."

Kate crawled into the back seat of the midnight-blue Lexus, while her energetic friend tossed the heavy luggage into the cluttered truck. Dana jumped into the driver's seat, adjusted the mirror, and buckled her seat belt. Kate complained about her miserable headache and Dana gave her a bottle of water and two aspirins. By the time they got onto Interstate 95, the pills kicked in and Kate finally relaxed. She munched on crispy mesquite chips, digging in for more but then stopping herself. She thought about 9/11, and why her cat had picked the worst time to die, and she thought about why Allie was punishing her.

In Connecticut, they passed Darien and Greenwich, and were approaching New Canaan, when Kate said she was getting hungry. The three-hour trip to Newport placed demands on their empty stomachs and tired heads. A McDonald's came into view—crispy French fries, a Big Mac cheeseburger oozing in juices and cheese, and hot tea sounded delicious on a cool September night. Like a kid, Kate talked about French fries as Dana drove into the parking lot.

Dana parked the car and turned off the engine. She opened the back door for Kate, who was sprawled out on the back seat, and said, "Get up, sweetie. Nirvana is waiting for us. Let's think about fries smothered in ketchup and salt. Do you want your burger medium rare? Get your arse up! I'm starving!"

Kate stretched her arms and yawned. She followed Dana past the church-like yellow arches on the doors to the smell of burgers and fries. They stopped at the toilette before queuing up for their orders. After receiving their food, they marched over to a vacant table, feeling blessed. They tossed the leftover fries back into the bags as extra snacks for the long trip ahead.

The scenery darkened under the nighttime sky. Kate sat in the front seat, listening to Dana chattering about her favorite topic—men. For the next half hour, she gave a lecture on how to trap them at the boat show or the bars. The conversation expanded like a helium balloon.

"Wear that sexy black dress with the low-cut back and the crisscross front, Kate," Dana counseled. "Put on your makeup! Men are suckers for model types and girls in their early twenties. And you look good enough to compete with those prima donnas. Remember, marriage is a great way to supplement your finances."

Kate snapped back, "Easy for you to give me advice when you don't have to worry about money, with your rich parents subsidizing your boutique."

"Sure, I have the shop, and my parents have some investments and money, but business is on and off. New York might get bombed again, and no building is safe. Anyway, I'm thinking about moving out of New York. I hope to buy a house and rent out some of the rooms; the additional income will help pay the mortgage and taxes. Would you be interested in co-investing or renting out a room?"

"Oh, Dana, you know that I have limited savings and have debt up the wazoo. And I'm too nervous to learn to drive. Even if I weren't, the insurance payments would set me back financially. Plus, I hate the boonies—they're swarming with married folks with kids."

Dana preached on, explaining the benefits of real estate investment in areas safer than New York. "Besides," she said, "more singles are starting to move to the 'burbs."

The topic of money exasperated Kate, and like a vendetta, her headache returned. She told her friend as tactfully as she could that she didn't want to discuss the future while on holiday time, and Dana finally shut up.

Their car approached an underpass draped in an American flag on its eastern side. Several people waved candles

144

to those who passed. Kate remembered that she had packed a white tea candle and rummaged through her bag. She asked Dana to honk the horn before they went under.

Dana pressed the horn several times. From the corner of her eye, she caught her friend placing a candle on the dashboard. She persuaded Kate not to do this, insisting that the car was no place for a memorial candle and she didn't want any burn spots on the upholstery.

Kate placed the candle back in the plastic bag. She sealed it shut and tucked it into one of the compartments in her bag. She looked dejected, gazing straight ahead, as time passed like the scenery outside.

Dana observed her friend's behavior, and said, "Kate, please understand that I'm only trying to be practical. What if the candle slipped and landed in your lap? You'd be one hot chick without a date. If you want to get burned, wait until we hit the bars. You can tell one of the schmucks to kiss your ass."

"Are you trying to convince me of the probability of my not finding anyone?" retorted Kate. "For all your expertise on men, I can't say much for your ability to hold on to them. As for me, you know damn well about my track record and how I feel about dating."

Dana decided to be quiet, and turned on the radio, hoping to defuse the compressed tension. The songs being played served as reminders of the recent tragedy, and the deejays were cautious about interjecting humor. While listening to the music, Dana admitted that she had lost control over her future.

145

Kate asked if she would mind if she switched to a jazz or classical station. Kate also reminded her about the cassettes and CDs in the glove compartment. Dana thanked her and pulled out a selection for her friend to choose from as they drove past the quaint landscape of Mystic, Connecticut.

*

Once Kate and Dana settled into their room at the bed and breakfast, the Carriage House Inn, they freshened up and applied a hint of blush and lipstick to their faces. They put on simple cotton Ann Taylor dresses. Before dashing out, they sprayed a little Crabtree & Evelyn Summer Hill eau de toilette. In the car, Dana suggested eating at Rosie's Bar and Grill, a fun tiki bar, for their first night in Newport. They could eat at a fancier place the following night.

When they arrived, Frank Sinatra's "New York, New York" was filling the air. Kate watched a desperate Dana scan for fresh opportunities at the teakwood bar.

"Kate, the pickings are too slim here," said Dana. "To spot one businessman among the college crowd is like finding that rusty old needle in some aging proverbial haystack. That haystack has probably become fertilizer. Should we give love the old college try?"

Kate couldn't offer advice because Dana had obviously left her street smarts back in New York, as well as her Clinique eyeliner during the security search.

146

Another stanza of "New York, New York" permeated the bar. Laughing strangers were oblivious to Kate, and she felt lost at this singles' luau. A few hormonal pimples marked her face, and her fingers tightened around the stem of her wine glass, imagining Allie's revenge.

Dana started a conversation with one of the college blockheads in a manner that sounded alien to Kate. This was not the Dana she knew; her charm and allure were going off limits tonight. Her friend's voice became unusually loud while ogling the young stud, Anthony, who bragged about himself, his new yacht, and his father's old one. Drunk from too many beers, he sucked face with Dana, the older woman. When Dana finished her Cabernet Sauvignon, she ordered another one to give herself a more youthful spunk, and Anthony paid for it.

Kate couldn't abandon Dana, no matter how idiotic she was acting, and took a few extra sips of Merlot for courage and cramps control. But the alcohol just added more blue to her blues. She dug her heels into the plush maroon carpeting and tried to disappear. She pressed her body against the wall by the parlor palm, but the plant wasn't large enough to hide her. Like Kate, the tree stood purely for decoration. A trio of laughing young women invaded her space. Kate fought back her tears and won.

She gulped down the wine and went for a refill. She passed ghost-like through the crowd of laughter. After ordering another Merlot, she returned to the palm tree. She sipped her wine and checked her watch, wondering when the hell their table would be ready.

Anthony spotted Kate, and his friend, Jared, joined him and Dana. Anthony nudged his buddy to check out the wallflower by the palm tree. Dana heard them but did nothing to interfere. Her mind began to waste away on the third glass of wine, and upon finishing it, she ordered a fourth.

Jared trapped his bait and asked Kate why she had such a glum look on her face. After being told to smile, Kate lashed back at his insensitivity, explaining that she came from New York City, where the towers had fallen.

Jared apologized for offending Kate. He retracted from his animal instinct and wished her a nice weekend. Kate backed down from her tirade and wished him the same. She ended their confrontation without an epilogue. Jared went to the men's room, and Kate escorted her tipsy friend to their reserved table.

One of the cheerful waitresses, wearing a name tag on her chest that said *Betty,* came to their table. Kate ordered the Porterhouse Steak Special for herself, the monkfish for Dana, and the jumbo shrimp appetizer for them to share. *No alcohol but espresso, pronto;* she wanted her inebriated friend to transform back to her old self as soon as possible. Plastic cards would cover tonight's damage, and calories would not be accounted for. Kate's mind turned to food as her comfort zone, her major reason for being in Newport.

The espresso arrived—instant caffeine gratification for born-again teetotalers. Dana relaxed and regained her

148

composure, chewing on the complimentary garlic and roasted tomato pita triangles. The appetizer and entrées followed, and both women sampled portions from each other's plates.

After the main course, Betty delivered the much-acclaimed dessert and cappuccino.

A revitalized Dana returned to her favorite topic, *men— how to trap one and get hitched, because there are too many fish in the sea*, before scooping into the chocolate dessert.

Kate listened, recalling the stench from the crates outside one of the fish stores in Astoria. It was clear that Dana did not have the credentials to write a book called *Getting a Man for Dummies*. Dana was good at catching fresh fish but couldn't hold on to her slippery partners after spending a few nights with them. Since the dessert appealed to Kate more than 'fresh fish' did, she happily dug her fork into the soft-textured center of the devil's food cake, oozing with chocolate mousse, and took a generous bite of chocolate orgasm. She looked at her watch, which read 9:29. If they were going to hop from one mansion to another tomorrow, sleep would have to take precedence over getting laid by imaginary prospects. She motioned to Betty for the check.

Chapter 15

Kate
(2001)

The next day, Kate and Dana strolled along Bellevue Avenue. Like children on their first trip to Disney World, their eyes feasted on the gaudy mansions. For ten dollars, Kate and Dana went on a fantasy tour at Rosecliff.

Room by room, a handsome tour guide named Charles ushered the group through the manor designed by Stanford White, who had brought the majesty of Versailles' Grand Trianon to Newport. He related the history of Rosecliff. Kate and Dana learned about the life of Theresa Fair Oelrichs, the daughter of Nevada silver "new money," who commissioned Stanford White to build her dream palace in 1898. The movies *High Society* and *The Great Gatsby* had been shot on the premises.

As Charles led them into the ballroom, a sudden chill rolled up Kate's legs. She blamed it on the open doorway to the lawn. From the corner of Kate's left eye, she saw a pale shadow pass under the window. She attempted to get her friend's attention, but Dana ignored her, giving her full attention to the tour guide.

The chills persisted. From across the room, Kate's cramps worsened and at that moment her life lost all logic. Dana finally noticed Kate's distress and took her outside for air, and Kate sat down and rested on a vacant stone bench.

The ocean waves crashed and the green acreage of Rosecliff framed its edges. Kate closed her eyes and took in her surroundings. How she wished that she could drown Allie in one of the massive waves. Like a shadow, Allie had walked across the Queensboro Bridge and followed her to Rosecliff. Allie didn't need to communicate in dreams or through the Ouija board; Kate feared that Allie now possessed her. And she was more eager than ever to contact Sarah to find out more about her 'Allie connection.'

She breathed in and realized that she was not alone.

Allie stood by, and said, "Kate, you are in grave danger and will die if you don't listen to me."

"What do you mean?" implored Kate.

Dana, who was sitting next to Kate, asked her what she was mumbling about. Kate opened her eyes, and Dana placed her hand on her shoulder, wondering if her friend was okay. Goosebumps covered Kate's arms. Dana pulled a bottle of ginger ale out of her backpack and offered it to Kate.

The soda revived her, and fifteen minutes later she was ready for a vigorous stroll along Cliff Walk. Its panorama conjured memories for Kate. She recalled her visit to San Francisco when she was twenty. She couldn't drive, and her ex-boyfriend, Steve Cox, had dumped her after they'd rented a car for the day. She remembered the seventeen-mile drive along the Pacific coastline and how Steve became sexually aggressive

151

when they stopped to take in the scenery. Now she observed the waves crashing against the rocks, while sailboats and yachts sailed by, trees thrived, roses stood like pruned princesses, and seagulls flew unrestricted. Here in Newport, life went on, seemingly oblivious to recent calamities or what Steve had tried to do to her.

The walk relieved her menstrual cramps and the nautical air added color to her complexion. She stopped to drink in the world around her. Every moment had to be made sacred. She entered a state of Zen, and then stumbled on a pebble. She turned around, and Dana was nowhere in sight. She panicked, afraid that Allie had caused something to happen. She traced her steps back and found Dana with a male tourist who, she learned, was from Georgia. Dana apologized and rejoined Kate for the duration.

After their walk, the women hopped into the Lexus and cruised along Bellevue Avenue to take in another popular tourist activity—shopping. The women stopped at a red light. As the light changed, sirens screamed, and Dana hit the brakes. Someone tapped Kate's shoulder, but it wasn't Dana. *It had to be Allie!* Kate's heart began to pump madly and she had difficulty breathing. Her hands covered her face as she tried to shield herself. After the fire truck passed, the tapping stopped, and Kate regained her senses.

She said, "It's like we never left New York," and began to cry.

Dana rubbed her shoulders, cooing, "Kate, it's okay to cry. I hate it when assholes tell you to be strong, until all the aches and pains eat you up. Girlfriend, we need to do some major shopping and split a bottle of wine over a big plate of Rhode Island seafood."

*

After coming back from the restaurant, Dana plopped herself on the sofa and fell asleep. Kate couldn't sleep because the third glass of wine still taunted her head. Her friend snored on, undisturbed, like an REM buzz saw. Not even an earthquake or bomb could wake her. Kate found the aspirin container on the counter and took a cup from the closet over the sink, rinsed it several times, and filled it with tap water.

Twelve minutes elapsed after washing down the pain reliever, but the aspirin lost the war against her headache. Kate searched through the complimentary beverage rack for chamomile or peppermint tea but only found Red Zinger. She immersed the tea bag in the boiling water. Her impatience brewed for three minutes, and she took a few sips, which burned the roof of her mouth.

Kate left the kitchenette, catching a glimpse of Dana sprawled out on the blue sofa. She walked past the snores toward the bedroom, where she would have the king-sized bed all to herself. After placing the hot beverage on the nightstand, she fell backward on the patchwork bedspread. Tomorrow they would be checking out of the Carriage House Inn before noon, and on Monday, it would be back to work, loneliness, and insecurity.

153

She closed her eyes and thought about the wasted time and money she had spent looking for a mate. The sexy little black dress remained untouched like a virgin, hiding inside an unzipped garment bag. She had dragged it out for nothing—they had both worn tank tops and capris to Ricky's Place on Thames Street. She recalled the two thirty-something couples at their table. They had an aura of self-assurance as they bragged about their jobs at Boston Interface Marketing. They discussed their trip to India and Nepal, and about Hinduism and Buddhism. Dana and Kate knew nothing about chakras and meditation; their topics of conversation centered on men, clothes, makeup, and work. Dana's points of reference usually included the tri-state bedrooms of local jocks disappearing like subway trains in the morning. Everyone shared farewells, but no one exchanged phone numbers, emails, or addresses.

Kate wondered about Dana's future plans. She guessed that 'Pollyanna' would continue to cover up her misery with promiscuity, although right now she was lying like a heap of laundry on the sofa. Tonight they had faked having a good time until the check came. At least the observant waiter did not charge Dana and Kate for the dessert. *How sweet of him! Sometimes pity did work in their favor.*

After finishing her tea, Kate washed the cup, dried it, and placed it back in the cupboard. Her headache subsided a little, and she managed to wash her face and brush her teeth but decided to defer her shower until early the next morning. She went into the bedroom and turned off the light. Still in her tank top and capris, she collapsed on the spacious bed, exhausted.

As darkness filled the room, Kate closed her eyes. After a while, she turned on her side in order to reach the glass of water next to her. Her hand reached over to turn on the nightstand lamp, but the bulb was missing from its socket. Kate sank her feet into her slippers and gingerly crept to the bathroom. The light switch and the bulbs over the sink were missing. She tried flicking the switches in the living room, foyer, and kitchenette, but none of them worked. Her tea candle shed light on the counter, but who had lit it? Maybe Dana? But where was she?

She carefully placed the candle on a dish and hunted for Dana, who was no longer on the sofa, nor was she anywhere. Kate checked the rooms again, calling out her friend's name but got no answer. Like the electricity, luggage, and furniture outside her bedroom, Dana had disappeared.

Once downstairs, Kate realized that the Carriage House Inn on Bull Street had been boarded up, except for the entrance to where she and Dana were staying. She noticed that Dana's Lexus had disappeared from the driveway. Kate had been left on her own, without money, identification, credit cards, or luggage.

As she turned the corner, she smelled something rancid. When she got closer, she saw a mutilated calico kitten lying in the gutter near a lamppost, perhaps the victim of a hit-and-run driver. Her stomach tightened when she realized that the kitten looked a lot like Amber. As she got closer, she saw her stuffed

155

animal Chloe again. She wondered how this could be when she had left Chloe on her bedroom shelf back at her father's house, and how could a stuffed animal smell like a dead cat? The sight and smell made Kate want to vomit.

Kate ran in the opposite direction, away from the toy. She found herself at the docks, where the bright lights along the wharf dimmed and the street sign suddenly disappeared. Like the Carriage House Inn, all the stores and eateries had been boarded up.

She heard moaning and saw a little girl in a blue and white dress sitting on the dock, holding the toy last seen on Bull Street. It was Allie.

With her face wet with tears and her frock stained in blood, Allie hugged the mangled stuffed animal like a real cat. She looked up at Kate and cried, "You shouldn't have left Amber in the driveway. Because of you, Dana couldn't have fun and had to pack up and leave, but as she drove off, she accidentally killed Amber. It's your fault that Amber's dead."

Kate shouted back, "First of all, this kitty is a toy, my toy, Chloe, not Amber. Second, how did the Carriage House Inn become a vacant, boarded-up shack without light and all its furniture gone, except in my room? Third, what happened to my personal belongings? And fourth, how could Dana suddenly leave, when I saw her sleeping on the sofa? By the way, Amber was my cat, not yours. Why do you hug this raggedy toy? Why do you continue to harass me?"

156

Allie pointed in the direction of the Sweetheart Novelty Company. Kate's belongings sat underneath the boarded-up window. Kate, aghast with disbelief, saw that her missing luggage and bags had reappeared. This had to be a dream, yet she couldn't wake up.

The child approached Kate and said, "I told you before that you must give the man who abducted me the happiness he craves in order to free me from him. But you refused to do it, and now my cat has died again. You will pay the price in the next few months. Your eggs will rot because you are a waste of womanhood. You're a disgrace to your parents. You can't even make it in the business world. People like you never marry, and they end up dying alone. You have found your soul mate in failure. The truth hurts, doesn't it, Kate? Have I opened more sores tonight?"

Kate tried yelling at Allie, but the child screamed out, "Kill me, Kate? How stupid can you be? I am dead! My uncle killed me when you were in diapers. I have always been older than you."

Since Kate was too furious to respond, Allie continued her diatribe. "Dear Kate, cat got your tongue?" Allie's smile widened and her eyes sharpened like the broken glass on the dock. Her rant continued. "Dear Kate, your refusal to write my story will not go unpunished. You were warned. This may just be a dream, but my words will come true."

She threw her head back in laughter as the mangled toy began to move, which did not seem to faze Allie, who squeezed

157

*its head with all her strength. The toy extended one front paw
and attempted to scratch her neck, letting out a powerful hiss.*

*The piercing noise angered the child and she tried to
break its neck, her hands sore from beating the toy and bleeding
from the scissor lacerations she had made. The claws of the
stuffed cat scratched Allie's right cheek. Allie tossed it into the
water and it sunk below, leaving dark ringlets of water to expand
and then disappear. In the distance, orange flames touched the
sky and the smell of smoke quickly approached the dock.*

Kate woke up in the king-sized bed and noticed that the
light on the nightstand was on and the luggage and the clothes
had never left the room. Everything seemed normal, except for a
flickering light outside the window, the acrid smell of smoke,
and the sirens boxing her eardrums.

Dana ran in, shouting, "Get up, Kate. The old oak tree in
the backyard across the way is on fire. Thank God it's not near
this house or the others. What a way to end this shitty vacation."

Kate pulled the blinds up and observed with horror that
the burning tree was an exact replica of the tree from her dreams.
Orange and yellow flames shot up from its branches, producing a
halo-like effect against the gray-blue sky. She heard crying
coming from the tree, the sounds of either a baby or a cat. She
hastily threw on a sweater and a pair of shorts, and dashed
downstairs. Dana darted across the lawn, but the police stopped
her. A woman from the house on the other side of the backyard
ran over to an officer, screaming, "Please save my Angel, my
little girl." Kate and Dana learned that the victim was the

missing calico cat posted on notices throughout the area. The animal, ten months old and very pregnant, resembled a mature Amber.

The cat sat on the lower branch, terrified, as orange flames burned relentlessly around her. Firemen arrived with a net, hose, and ladder, while bystanders stared. The cat's tearful mistress screamed for her "Angel" to jump down; however, the meowing cat stayed stock-still. A few flames singed her fur. The net drew nearer, but the cat jumped to a higher branch. The fire, hungry and fierce, worked its way toward her, until finally she leaped into the net, to the sound of relieved applause. A few seconds later, the fire swallowed the branch.

One of the firemen took the cat from the net and carried her over to her sobbing owner, Terry Reese. Angel's fur was scorched in several spots and her white front legs were still bleeding from being sheared.

Angel had left some of her blood on the tree's bark. Kate remembered the burning tree in her dreams that bled and moaned. The firemen quickly gave the cat first-aid, as the grateful owner thanked God for miraculously saving her beloved cat.

Allie, in a bloodied blue dress, emerged from the bushes, and Kate coaxed Dana to look, but Dana didn't see the child. Again, Kate pointed and pushed the branches aside, but only she saw the smirking child, who quickly disappeared when the flames extinguished into ghostly smoke.

Kate no longer dismissed her dreams as a place for emotional release. She was frightened by Allie's predictions, the beaten and singed cat doll, and the burning tree that paralleled the real one she'd witnessed tonight. Allie played mind games as a form of punishment. She wanted—no, needed—her story to be told, as if it were crucial that she be remembered. Her life had ended tragically, and the disfigured man had denied her a happy afterlife. Kate's abstinence from giving him sex made Allie's dilemma worse. She wondered why she dreamt about having sex with him. She even debated whether she was somewhat fascinated with him. By having sex with him, he would be satisfied, and Allie could return to a blissful afterlife. Kate still had Allie's story on her computer and planned to finish it. Once these two tasks were accomplished, Kate would, hopefully, be free.

Kate and Dana went upstairs, and in a few hours the area became quiet. But the smell of the tree's death lingered in the morning air.

*

The two New Yorkers rose at 8:15, finished packing, and paid Maria Pasadena the bill. They exchanged farewells before slamming the trunk of the Lexus shut. Maria waved as the homeward-bound car departed.

With Dana in a chatty mood again, Kate rested her head against the back seat and thought about the grotesque and savage dreams. As she gazed at the passing scenery, she vowed to call Sarah as soon as she got home. She desperately needed to talk to

160

someone who had shared the same dreams. She hoped that Sarah checked her messages while on vacation.

Kate didn't want to face her fate alone.

Chapter 16

Kate
(2001)

Kate made a last-minute decision that instead of returning to Brooklyn she would call her father before she left the Carriage House Inn and ask to stay over again at his place. Dana offered to drive her to Astoria, but Kate said no. She didn't want to tell Dana the truth—that she had to get away from her non-stop mouth. Kate asked Dana to drop her off by the New York Public Library on Fifth Avenue, where she would catch a cab and take in the glamour of the City before crossing the Queensboro Bridge into Queens.

Through the taxi window, the urban streets of Manhattan moved like stills from a film. The fashionable boutiques along Madison Avenue illuminated at dusk. A few restaurants stayed open for business. Carefree sophistication still lured singles like her to be part of this bouillabaisse lifestyle. Yet Kate knew that something was amiss. The restaurants were as empty as the streets—as if people had walked across bridges and never come back. The mannequins along Madison were dressed in winter fashions—Kate thought that they were the lucky ones. Devoid of emotions, they would never be disturbed by dreams, nor would they ruminate about love, work, or the world.

The cab crossed the Queensboro Bridge into Long Island City. Grayish-blue tints covered the bridge and buildings on both sides of the East River. The bridge spanned in semi-darkness, with the major skyscrapers like the Empire State and Chrysler Buildings dimmed. Color-coded alerts became the new trend, with orange being the primary hue.

Silence muted all conversation until the taxi turned onto Northern Boulevard, at which point the cabbie began venting about 9/11 and the Muslims. Kate sat with her jaws firmly clamped as the cabbie praised Dubya and Giuliani for *doing such a great job down at Ground Zero.* He predicted that Bush would be re-elected and the mayor would be the next president after Bush finished his second term.

Kate elected silence. This tirade might as well be taking place at her father's house. Kate tried to hold her fire; she didn't have the strength to argue with a bigot. The driver rambled on, expressing his nihilistic outlook for America, as his passenger drifted inward.

Kate had lost Brent and her need for love and kids in a post–9/11 world. Amber had come and gone. Like her period, the bills came monthly, but unlike the bills, her period became erratic, and this month, a bit too scanty.

The driver ranted on about potential bombings of airports, subways, and buildings throughout the New York area, across America, and the Western World.

Kate thought about her handful of friends; she could do without their silliness. She would have to face her father. She

163

would have to call Sarah and discuss the Allie dreams. She would have to screw with the enemy who held Allie captive.

The driver was now lecturing about reservoirs being sabotaged, germ warfare contaminating crops, and gas bombs in subways. Kate shrank against the torn leather seat.

The cab parked near the driveway of Mr. Robbins's modest brick two-story dwelling. The familiar rosebushes stood in bloom next to the garbage cans. But the street appeared different, an unnatural hush hitting her as she crawled out of the cab. The ubiquitous American flag adorned cars, windows, and lawns. A few lit candles stood like sentries on the steps of houses across the street. Nighttime welcomed her back to her childhood home, but it didn't feel like home.

She handed the cabbie a crisp twenty, plus three crumpled singles. He thanked her, flashing a yellow-toothed smile. Her generous tip turned him into an obsequious gent, jumping out of the cab to assist her with the luggage. He even offered to carry her bags to the doorstep. She refused, hoping he would disappear. He wished her a good night before driving away. Soon the block became dark and quiet, and Kate preferred it this way. She dragged her luggage along the walkway, up the four concrete steps. Waiting to hear her father's voice on the intercom, she rang the bell—the stranger who returned as his daughter.

*

Kate and her father had established a truce after the dispute about her lifestyle this past Tuesday. Her old man's yelp was worse than his bite. Coming back to Astoria made her hungry. She microwaved a frozen pizza for dinner and had vanilla ice cream for dessert. After dinner, she unpacked her luggage in her old room. The room looked exactly the same as it had when she moved out, after her mother's death, with pale yellow walls, ecru lace drapes, and green and pink floral bedspread. The dolls and stuffed animals wore benevolent expressions. Her eyes fixed on her calico cat doll, Chloe, whole and unharmed. She gave her a special hug before placing her back on the shelf. Kate's dirty underwear and clothes lay in a plastic bag. She wouldn't wash them until she returned to Brooklyn on Tuesday.

She took a quick shower and brushed her teeth. Tomorrow was Monday. Although she had completed her assignments on Friday, Kate sensed that they might not meet with Jackie's approval. Exhausted from the strange vacation, she turned off the light, temporarily forgetting about life in general and her boss in particular, and fell into a dreamless sleep.

165

Chapter 17

Kate
(2001)

On Monday morning, Kate arrived at work early. She casually ate her blueberry muffin and drank her coffee. She was able to eat her breakfast in peace, without the disturbance of new emails, voicemails, or incoming calls. A few co-workers passed by and said hello. When some inquired about her weekend, Kate lied and said she had a great time.

At ten, Jackie arrived but didn't say hello as she passed by Kate's cubbyhole. However, she smiled and greeted the other employees.

Minutes later, the light flashed on her phone and Kate answered it. Through the speaker, she heard her boss say, "Kate, I need to speak to you *now!*" Those eight discouraging words could mean anything, stemming from the known fact that Jackie was inclined to execute vitriolic lectures, and today her voice sounded even more ominous than usual. Kate carefully returned the receiver to its cradle, knowing that a slam would only feed her boss's wrath.

Torn between obedience and defiance, Kate leaned toward walking out, but as a slave to her paycheck, she couldn't, since her stellar résumés had either been filed in the garbage or lost in cyberspace. Her nerves began to wreak havoc with her stomach, and a portion of her digested breakfast came up in her mouth. As her palpitations increased, her courage disintegrated. Beads of sweat formed on her forehead as she knocked on Jackie's door.

Jackie heard two knocks and figured, *why rush the tension when she could let it simmer a bit.* Two more knocks followed, and another minute passed before Jackie opened the door.

Jackie told Kate to come in and ushered her to one of the plush chairs. Her business etiquette came straight out of the freezer. Jackie returned to her chair, ready for the kill.

With bad omens in motion, Kate wondered if Jackie was about to fire her. She stiffened in the chair and the upholstery hardened beneath her buttocks, as the executioner in her red Donna Karan suit straightened her posture.

Jackie's lips narrowed as she spoke. "Kate, you've been making too many errors lately, and when it's pointed out to you, you go into one of your infamous temper tantrums. You're older than me—I assume you're almost forty—but you behave like a four-year-old."

"I only express my disagreement in a rational manner, and my age is a private matter," retorted Kate.

"I've been receiving reports from others that you make them feel uncomfortable," stated Jackie. Her eyes targeted the squirming Kate, and she waited for her subordinate to respond.

"Excuse me, Jackie?" said Kate. "I don't know what you're talking about."

167

Jackie adjusted her red frames as she leaned forward and said, "You don't know what I'm talking about? I've witnessed your disruptive attitude toward your peers on several occasions. Your chronic nastiness and slamming things on your desk, including your phone, have created a hostile environment, and others find you unapproachable. In the business world, we must learn to work together as a team and not be controlled by our emotions."

"That's an exaggeration, Jackie! I get along quite well with everyone, and Ellen Price is my best friend."

"Kate, I'm well aware that she's your closest friend and only ally here. But you're making the rest of the team nervous, especially now with those loud conversations with your father. I understand you've temporarily moved back to Astoria. Living with an aging parent can be difficult. Kate, your personal life is interfering with your career."

"Jackie, I don't speak loudly. I hear conversations from others down the hall and never complain about it. Besides, I have a strong, able-bodied father who is active with his church and his pals from the police force. As a matter of fact, he will be driving me home to my apartment tonight."

"Kate, let me cut to the chase," interrupted Jackie. "A co-worker has filed a report against you, and you and I have an appointment with Human Resources at two."

"What? Why didn't they confront me directly?"

"Kate, the name of the person is not important, but the action itself is serious enough to require HR's attention."

Kate wanted to scream. This had to be one of Allie's predictions—*Me finding my soul mate in failure?* She protested. "What are my rights when I'm being falsely accused of misconduct? A little understanding, please. I just lost a dear friend on 9/11, and my stomach is giving me trouble today."

Jackie paused before resuming, using a softer approach, admitting that this meeting might just be a warning. She offered to treat Kate to something that would settle her stomach, like chamomile tea and toast. She dialed Java Muffin and placed the order, and threw in a Cobb salad with low-fat Italian dressing and a Diet Snapple iced tea for herself.

Kate kept her thoughts to herself. Jackie had demolished her, and now she was acting like an altruistic friend. *Jackie Friedman was calling for her secretary's last meal before her execution, and how generous of her to pay for it.* Kate thought of how much she wanted to shove the tea and toast up Jackie's fancy anal-retentive crack. But how could she when her only option for employment had collapsed with the North Tower?

Jackie dismissed Kate and promised to call her when the food arrived. Kate thanked her, thinking, *fuck you and Allie too!*

Meanwhile, Jackie watched her subordinate exit and thought, *Yeah, swallow your pride and eat your words too, my dear!*

Jackie immediately closed the door, making sure she had pressed the button on lock. She dialed Susan Rhodes to ask if Kate's "warning documents" were ready for the two o'clock meeting. Jackie added that 'we have another winner here,

169

reminiscent of Sarah Kahn and only slightly less weird.' What a coincidence that Kate and Sarah knew each other, and that Kate had tried to get it on with Brent before 9/11and his tragic death.

When Susan answered *yes* to having the papers ready, Jackie asked her whether Ellen Price deserved something in her paycheck for her cooperation, and Susan agreed that it was a good idea. The HR director also accepted an invitation to join Jill Myers, the copy director from Steinberger's, and Jackie for drinks and dinner tonight at seven at a new place called Simon's on Columbus Avenue.

*

On the trip back to Brooklyn, Kate didn't tell her father that she might lose her job at Focus NYC; she was too embarrassed and distraught to go from A to Z with the details. After her father carried the luggage upstairs to her apartment and kissed her goodbye, Kate noticed that there were two messages on her answering machine; one from her roommate, Anne, and the other from Dana. According to Anne's message, she did return from Italy but decided to leave the apartment to stay over at her boyfriend, Eddie Valenti's, Tudor-style home in Bay Ridge, Brooklyn, for a week. Dana's message asked Kate not to call her until tomorrow, because she wouldn't be back from her date until late tonight. Kate erased both messages.

She sat on her bed, feeling boxed in by her day of defeat. Eight hours ago, she had signed the papers in HR, agreeing to the terms of the warning. She had to sacrifice her self-esteem to keep her thankless job. She pondered which was more painful, the false accusations or her inability to fight back.

Alone in the apartment, Kate suddenly had a sense of foreboding. She desperately wanted to talk with Dana and left an urgent message for her to call. Only Sarah could shed some light on the Allie connection. She left an extensive message for Sarah, hoping to rekindle the friendship. She left her phone number, as well as Dana's. She also tried Jen, but she too was unavailable. Again, she left her number, as well as Dana's.

She had lost her appetite and prepared for bed instead, forgoing her nightly shower. Once in bed, she tossed from side to side. She didn't fall asleep until three a.m.

*

Kate's bedroom had no walls, lamps, throw rugs, furniture, or other possessions, with the exception of her bed, floral sheets, lilac pillow, and cover. Foliage replaced the contents of her room, as well as the rest of her apartment. Shades of gray-blue unveiled mysticism and wonder, and her curiosity lured her from her bed. No longer afraid, she would do whatever Allie commanded her to do. She walked into the wilderness. The dew of the forest and the aroma from both the exotic and ordinary flowers hypnotized her. She walked deeper into the trance and deeper still into the forest. She felt light on her feet—her leg muscles now loose and limber. The crickets played nocturnal sonatas as she passed by, sending her further into a semi-conscious state. Her mind emptied, and she walked in neither pain nor pleasure, nor in peace of mind.

171

She saw the tree that was once on fire. Still bleeding from its wounds, it moaned and shed tears. She extended her fingers and touched the wet bark. She tasted the salty blood on her fingertips. The blood continued to flow down the lower bark. Kate investigated further and recognized the scent—her menstrual blood. She backed away, crinkling her nose. Her stomach muscles winced and she groaned in pain.

From the bushes, someone watched her movements. Kate saw the ten-year-old girl in her blue and white dress. Like arrows, the girl's almond-brown eyes fixed on Kate; they seemed to be shouting 'cat murderer.' Pain pounded Kate's stomach like a drum.

Before Kate could deny the charges, Allie reiterated her allegation and pointed her finger, seeming to mock her. "Dear Kate, cat got your tongue again? You've never cared about anyone but yourself. I've asked for your help in sending me back where I belong, but you have refused. Dear Kate, I must follow you everywhere until I am free from this pit. I guess you didn't care for my stories, because you stopped writing them on your computer. Did you know that Sarah, yes, Kate, your former friend, almost trashed my stories because she got annoyed at me? But she finally listened."

Grabbing a fallen branch, Kate shouted, "So why do you need me for your tasks when you have Sarah? Why are you putting the onus on me? I ought to beat your ass red."

Allie went on, trying to persuade Kate that she was a better writer than Sarah, and that Allie's captor found Kate

172

more attractive. The child reminded her again that she needed
her help because she had been abducted from her beautiful room
in the afterlife. She described her room as being filled with toys,
books, and pretty things. Her walls and curtains had been
painted a lemony yellow, and a pink and yellow floral bedspread
covered her bed. Her window seat overlooked a garden. Her
abductor craved the kind of love that she, being a child, couldn't
possibly give. Because he needed his manhood to be pacified, he
would beat her whenever he became angry. Allie begged Kate
not to refuse him; that perhaps she might learn to enjoy it and
even fall in love. Sarah did and it had changed her life for the
better. Should Kate continue to refuse, though, she would face
dire consequences, especially now that her love life, job, and
health were in jeopardy.

The walls of Kate's uterus swelled and she moaned as
the pain traveled to her chest. She wanted to wake up, but Allie
had full control now.

Allie paused for a moment and then went on speaking. "I
don't mean to sound so harsh. I forgive you for what happened
to my cat, Amber, even though you had her barbecued over the
fire."

"She was not barbecued," Kate corrected. "I buried her
in my backyard."

Allie buried her head in the crease of Kate's chest, but
Kate pushed her away. From out of nowhere, a pair of hands
cupped Kate's breasts. Fingers massaged them, calming Kate
with each circular stroke. The buttons on her nightie dropped

173

one by one as fingers worked their magic on her flesh. She
smiled as the hands moved upward and stroked her hair. She
saw Allie watching by the bushes and reflected on what the child
had said. Kate's hostility toward her nemesis turned to
tenderness. Her breasts became fuller and her nipples enlarged
and leaked with milk. A surge of maternal love flowed from Kate
like her breast milk.

The gentle fingers caressed, igniting Kate's passion. She
turned around and saw Brent's naked body—he was alive. Like a
kitten, he kneaded her for milk. A rush of hormones sent a warm
sensation between her legs because the doors to her virginity
needed to be broken.

Brent smiled and said nothing as Allie sat stone-faced by
the bushes, staring at Kate. Kate looked away and concentrated
on the foreplay, desiring sexual baptism. The child moved to sit
on a nearby rock for a closer look. Kate removed her panties,
and at the same time, a breeze tickled Kate's flesh. Feeling
sensuous, she dropped her remaining garment as she ambled
toward the pond, leaving her inhibitions discarded like her
clothes. She was no longer aware of Allie's presence. Kate
submerged into the pond and watched her reflection disappear.
Brent observed her from the rosebush. Allie handed him a tiny
flask and he placed it down by the edge of the pond.

The muddy pond smelled rancid. She moved to the end of
it, where the mud thickened. She washed in it, rubbing the soft
earth and rough pebbles into her hair and skin. It stimulated her
dormant desires and exfoliated her inhibitions once again, and

174

the stench aroused her further. Her nipples hardened as Brent drew nearer. She smiled and lay down on the wet soil, allowing him to massage her. His hands rubbed the mud all over her hair, face, and neck. She screamed for more.

But once his hands reached her breasts, they became deformed and callused. Like knives, his nails cut into her flesh. He smacked her, once, twice, and thrice across her face. He pushed Kate into the mud. Brent's handsome face turned grotesque, as his jagged nails mauled the skin around her areolas.

Kate kicked him in the groin, but he was stronger, and he punched her in the stomach. She yelled out in excruciating pain as he slapped her harder. He grabbed the flask, bit off the top, and spit out the seal. He shoved the opened flask between Kate's lips and poured the rotten-smelling solution down her throat. She shook violently as some of the liquid leaked from her mouth. He placed his thin blue lips on her nipples and repeatedly kissed them. The sensation soothed her as the foul potion slowly began lulling her into semi-consciousness. She fell backward, landing on the soft earth. Her legs spread open in anticipation of his next move. The creature smiled and gently rubbed fresh mud into her open sores and vagina before his final move. Kate smiled too, enjoying this creature, even his ugliness. Her vagina now felt warm from his ejaculation and Kate didn't want it to end. Their passion exploded into hours. She drifted into inertia, her muscles temporarily free from pain as she progressed deeper into the dream.

Allie watched the two become lovers and it made her mad. She had lied to Kate about his treatment of her. He had never hurt her, even when he was angry. He had never once hit her. She knew he desired Kate more than anyone else. It should have been Allie underneath him, not Sarah and Kate. She found hidden beauty behind the creature's brown eyes. She loved him when he came and took her to his world. She followed him willingly into the forest because his eyes looked oddly familiar. He told her that he was John Martin, the middle-aged janitor at school who handed her tissues to dry her tears whenever she was having a bad day. He would share his sad stories. He would run to the pond, screaming for love. Those sessions would last for hours. She sat by his side, holding his hands. She loved kissing them. Her kisses always calmed him down. He would say, find me fresh meat. She found it unbearable to listen to his rants but knew eventually she would have to lure virgins for him. First Sarah, and now Kate. Unhappy women were easy prey, and Allie trapped them while they slept. She hunted down literary types, luring them in their dreams to write her mother's story, before bringing them to John. She would lie and say it was her story. Her mother probably didn't know that she had broken her promise to keep her story a secret. She had never cared for her mother. She blamed her for her dismal life on earth.

Allie never knew John's secrets until that first night in the forest. She learned that he had hated his diabetic mother, and women in general. His mother blamed him for her misery, and even for the death of his father. She would terrorize him with

176

the strap before locking him in the basement. As an adult, he lived at home, caring for his mother. Women called him a momma's boy, and he blamed his mother for his lonely life. When he doused the living room furniture with gasoline before tossing his lit cigarette at the sofa, he didn't realize that his mother had left the house ten minutes earlier. He carelessly dripped gasoline on his feet where the cigarette landed. He became a human matchstick, falling on the sofa while the house burned down with him in it. It was her beloved friend, John Martin, the janitor who died a few weeks before she herself was killed at the hands of her uncle.

Having lost John to Kate, Allie had to leave the forest, her home for more than thirty years. She saw the meadow ahead. With each step, she walked in hesitation. Once outside, she lifted her head in the falling rain. Soon the rain diminished to a shower. Allie stood, feeling the warm raindrops wash her skin, hair, and clothes. The wet dress tightened. The fabric hugged her emerging curves, arousing her. Buttons popped, seams ripped. Her body, no longer imprisoned by a child's blue and white dress, transformed into a woman's. With generous breasts and hips and tufts of hair under her armpits and between her legs, she lifted her arms upward, rejoicing in the rain. She ran toward the pond. In its reflection, she was naked and in love with herself. She wanted to jump in and swim. As she touched her hardening nipples, she cried out for John. In the distance, a rainbow graced the sky. She decided not to follow it. It would not lead her to happiness. She returned to the forest, allowing the thickets to close behind her.

*

Traces of gray-blue still draped Kate's bedroom, now intact and foliage-free. On Tuesday morning, the nightstand clock stopped at 4:10 a.m. The birds chirped again, happy troubadours for the approaching dawn. However, Kate didn't hear them as she lay on her bed, quiet and naked, her breasts covered with scratches, and her vagina, as well as her disheveled bed, covered in blood.

The morning became afternoon, and the afternoon became night. For the next few days and nights, Kate couldn't budge out of her bed. She did not know that Dana had left five messages on her answering machine. When Dana knocked on her door on Saturday, Kate couldn't answer. Dana panicked and asked the superintendent to unlock the door, as she had misplaced Kate's emergency keys. Both Dana and the super entered and called out Kate's name, but she couldn't answer. They thought they smelled rotting food from the kitchen. But the stench wasn't coming from the kitchen. They walked to the bathroom, but they realized that the reek was coming from behind the closed bedroom door. They knocked on the door, yelling for Kate to answer, but Kate couldn't hear them. When they opened the door, they found Kate lying on her bed with her mouth frozen in a silent scream. The superintendent made the sign of the cross before calling 9-1-1, as Dana fell to her knees in shock.

Chapter 18

Dana
(2010)

The lush backyard looked greener after the rain and the thick August humidity hung like an invisible vine over Brooklyn. A calico cat named Angel Fire cried by the doorway to Dana's backyard. Poor Angel Fire couldn't shed her fear of the garden on a cloudy day. Dana sat on her stone bench and said, "What's the matter, baby?" She extended her hand, waving a feather toy in front of her kitty. When the cat ran to her, Dana picked her up and rocked her in her arms, humming a made-up tune. She massaged her from head to tail, and back again. The warmth of her body calmed the cat.

Dana had been reading a story called *By Dave's Creek* to Angel Fire. Sarah had written this gothic tale for children under her nom de plume, *Madison Peters*. It took place in a dense garden, where the sky above was neither dawn nor dusk. The protagonist, Mina, a girl in a blue gingham dress etched in white lace, owned a calico kitten named Ginger. The evil man with no name wore a black hat and cape. He locked the girl and her cat in his stone tower by Dave's Creek. The girl and the cat had to perform three tasks to ensure their escape.

Dana didn't plan to have kids, as she was past forty, although these days it was not unusual for women of this so-called advanced age to bear children. Most were married, and some of them planned on keeping their careers, as long as they had help from a nanny or a stay-at-home husband. They proudly pushed their trophies all over Brownstone Brooklyn, as if to say, *look at me—I'm a mother*, while almost running over Dana's *single* toes. She had been tempted to buy a stroller and roam the streets with Angel Fire, shouting, *my kitty's better than your kiddie*. She kissed Angel Fire's head and handed her fur baby a treat.

Dana reminisced about Kate. Kate had brought Sarah and Jen back into the fold by leaving phone messages the night before she died. Kate had given them Dana's phone number as well as hers. With regard to the Allie dreams, it seemed that all the recipients were dateless, had writing abilities, and had once lived in the same Bronx apartment where Allie had lived. Sarah's files confirmed this. Sarah had been the other dream recipient, until she met and married Manny. Jen never had any of these dreams because she had always dated, and then married Steven Fein.

Dana had always dated, but her love life was currently at a standstill. *Funny how she had started dreaming of Allie, not as a child, but as an adult.* Had she, a non-writer, become the torchbearer of Allie's story, carrying on where Kate and Sarah left off? She mentioned these dreams to Sarah and Jen, and they suggested that she compare her notes with Kate's files. Sarah planned to share hers with Dana. And Jen, who worked as a senior editor in publishing, believed it would make a great book.

Dana believed that Kate never had many choices, and that had she survived the heart attack, she would still have been alone. Kate used to confide in Dana that she wanted to have kids before forty. She would never have been able to make it as a single mom, nor could she even make it in the business world. Not Kate. She lacked the will to fight, even in publishing her poems, although her dreams would have provided excellent material had she continued to write them. Dana wondered whether there was more she could have done to comfort her. Taurus girls like Kate tended to be damn stubborn, wanting to do things their way; however, Kate had lacked the street smarts of a Frank Sinatra.

Dana thought about her early retirement from the dating scene, which she took shortly after Kate died. She started to understand what Kate must have gone through and ended those silly games of Cat and Mouse vs. Boy Meets Girl. Dana's problems belonged to her, and why share them with someone else, and vice versa, with all those shitty marriages and even shittier divorces, and having kids would complicate things further. She'd heard enough stories from the 'stroller brigade' to fill the Library of Congress. Dana's future inheritance, her investments, and her shop, along with the added bonus of Social Security, would keep her financially secure for the rest of her life. She could go for in vitro fertilization and raise a family on her own. But a pet proved to be cheaper, offering unconditional love and never answering back.

181

While stroking the cat's head, she thought again of Kate and the horror of seeing her dead, the cops asking questions, and the EMS carrying her out on a stretcher, covered. Strange that Kate left this world with a slightly contorted smile. The police and the EMS ruled out rape because of the lack of semen and fingerprints indicative of an assault, plus her self-inflicted scratches and the fact that she had her period and wasn't wearing a tampon. Such an unhappy person deserved to die happy, but had she? Was it the dream that had brought on her sudden cardiac arrest? As far as Dana knew, Kate did not go for physicals. Although the autopsy stated that Kate had a congenital heart problem, did Allie actually kill her? She thought there might be clues hidden in her laptop. She wondered whether Kate had written about her life, assuming that she might have kept a literary journal or diary of her dreams. She was curious to read them, and maybe she could have them published in Kate's name and memory. She asked permission from Joe Robbins, Kate's father, but he wanted no part of it. A week later, he gave her the computer with all files intact.

Dana refused to move after Kate's death. Talking about suburbia had become a passing fantasy left behind in Newport. Anne moved some of her things out of 3B the same day Kate died. She decided to move in with Eddie, because the apartment felt too eerie for her to stay. Later that week, the rest of her items were either dumped or taken to her parents' house in Forest Hills. Apartment 3B soon became vacant, except for one. Dana walked into Kate's bedroom that evening. None of the lights

182

were on and the Venetian blinds remained drawn. She thought she saw a light by the window. When she came closer, it vanished. She wondered if Anne had had a similar encounter. She called her the next day and asked, and Anne said *no*.

After Kate's burial, Dana revisited the Carriage House Inn for a few days. She told Maria, the innkeeper, the awful news about her friend. Dana also inquired about Terry Reese, the lady whose pregnant cat had been stuck in the burning tree. Maria said that they found the two teenaged boys responsible for the arson attack. Angel had given birth to two kittens: one calico and the other a red tabby, although two others, another calico and a red and white tabby mix, were stillborn. Dana asked if she could adopt the calico, since this cat bore an uncanny resemblance to Amber, Kate's dead kitten. Terry agreed, but advised Dana to come back in April, when the kitten had finished weaning from its mother, Angel. Terry named her Angel Fire, to honor the kitten's mother.

Sometime before Christmas, Dana logged on to Kate's computer. She opened a file folder on the desktop labeled *The Allie Chronicles*. Her fingers froze on the keyboard, and she immediately shut down the computer for the night.

When the landlord, Allen Weinstein, put the dove-gray building up for sale, Dana saw it as a lucrative investment, and with the help of her parents, got a mortgage. Instead of moving to her cousin's house in Norwalk, or her parents' townhouse in Brooklyn Heights, she rented a studio nearby on Carroll Street. She sold her furniture and placed the rest of her possessions in storage. Extensive renovations were made, and Dana made sure that 3B and 4B were combined. Dana planned to make that apartment hers. She had to protect Kate from strangers—too many people had moved in and out of 3B. A former tenant, Bill Hansen, claimed to have seen a female apparition pacing the area between his converted office and the bathroom. Prior to the Big Recession, her shop, *Dana's,* gave her extra cash to liquidate her assets. Today, her merchandise didn't move unless it went on sale. More of her steady customers had to file for unemployment. She hoped President Obama could eventually lasso the economy's complicated domino effect. She still kept the *Change* poster in her office at the store. Although not in dire need of selling the store, she still worried about the future. She had been seeing too many businesses disappear throughout the City.

After the renovations, Dana decided to reopen the file folder labeled *The Allie Chronicles*. A slight chill came and went as a list of chapters appeared. The most recent file had been opened on September 8, 2001. She skimmed through the chapters, reading Allie's story, and rereading the violent content. She closed the documents one by one. Angel Fire watched Dana from her cat bed. She meowed loudly and banged her right paw on the floor. She hopped up on Dana's lap with paws extended on her owner's solar plexus, before hitting the keyboard several times. Her owner pulled her off, saying, "Angel Fire, not now, not yet. I need more time." The cat disobeyed and jumped back onto the keyboard. Dana picked the cat up by the scruff of her neck. Dana's brown eyes met the cat's amber ones, and she

184

whispered, "Another time, sweetie, another time." She kissed her before retiring for the night.

Dana placed her book down on the bench and temporarily relinquished her thoughts of Kate, *The Allie Chronicles*, and the economy, and focused instead on the natural beauty of her garden. Sunlight broke through the clouds, and blue hues replaced the sky's gray tints. The sunflowers stood tall against the dove-gray brownstone. Bright yellow-feathered petals radiated around brown centers. Like the white hydrangeas, the snapdragons' vivid red and white heads contrasted against shades of green. Everything looked brighter after the rain, and the smell of earth and greenery, rich and gentle. Honeysuckle vines blended with the scent. Dana meditated, taking in the beauty of her property. Angel Fire calmly walked past her. The cat liked being outdoors whenever the sun shone but never at dawn or dusk, and cloudy days were particularly problematic. Dana hugged Angel Fire again and offered her another treat.

*

The cat jumped off her lap and scurried over to her favorite bush for an afternoon nap. Dana stayed on the bench, thinking about Sarah; friend, author, and new tenant. There had been a vacancy in Apartment 3A, across from Dana's, this past January. Sarah and her husband, Manny Medina, lived in a tiny two-bedroom condo apartment near Brooklyn's Prospect Park, and they wanted more space and access to a backyard for their eight-year-old daughter, Emma. Before moving into Apartment 3A, they remodeled the kitchen. They redid the brown granite countertops with black granite and installed black appliances in place of the stainless steel ones. Cherry-finished cabinets replaced the light wooden ones. Dana learned to put up with the noise, while Angel Fire hid in the bathroom during construction. The Medinas moved in at the end of May, and Dana and Angel Fire enjoyed their freedom from the racket.

Manny, a tall second-generation Queens-born Puerto Rican, owned a chain of Mac support repair shops called iMedina, and made a dent in the photography world. Plain Sarah achieved almost model-perfect looks, with waist-length reddish-blonde hair; her taste now leaned toward the finer boutiques and spas. She wrote a children's book, *By Dave's Creek,* which Dana purchased and read to Angel Fire. Sarah preferred to use her nom de plume, *Madison Peters,* rather than *Sarah Medina.* The book had made *The New York Times* Best Seller List the previous Christmas; the story and artwork were reminiscent of Tim Burton's imaginative style. When Sarah autographed Dana's copy at her Barnes & Noble book event on Seventh Avenue in Brooklyn, she confided to her that she had gotten her ideas from the Allie dreams, but since it was a kid's book, she had to keep it G-rated.

Dana surmised that Allie favored Sarah over Kate. Sarah had gone on to a happy marriage and became an accomplished writer, while Kate had died a miserable failure in both her love life and her career.

Sarah and Manny's only child, Emma, attended a private school, the Berkeley Carroll School in Park Slope. She favored her handsome father in appearance and shared her mother's bookishness. Emma grew tall and excelled in her studies. She absorbed books like ice cream. Her personality would be best described as a sunflower. Even though the child was basically healthy, she had a functional heart murmur, which the doctors said she would outgrow in time. With no medication required, Emma could have a normal childhood.

Dana decided to ask Sarah and Jen over to study the journals and files at her apartment. Bringing husbands was optional. Jen's husband couldn't make it, since he would be at a medical convention in Chicago. Dana's assistant, Michelle, would mind the store that day. Dana grabbed Angel Fire and carried her upstairs. The cat jumped from her arms and ran up to the third floor, waiting for her mistress on the top step. Dana clapped her hands and Angel Fire dashed over, brushing her tail against her legs. The cat followed her over to 3A. As Dana rang the Medinas' bell, Angel Fire rolled over and washed her tail, making herself presentable for the neighbors.

Sarah opened the door and greeted her. "Hi, Dana. How are you?"

"Fine, Sarah. Would you, Manny, and Emma like to come over to my place for a Saturday afternoon get-together? We could finally review *The Allie Chronicles*, comparing your files, Kate's, and mine. You did mention this a few weeks ago. Jen plans to come without Steven, who will be doing his convention thing. Does three o'clock sound good? You know, we haven't seen Jen since April."

187

"That would be great, Dana. We have no plans for this weekend. And, actually, this weekend would be good, because we're leaving for Vancouver the following week, vacation-slash-wedding. Manny's baby sister, Theresa, is getting married."

Both Dana and Sarah said goodbye; however, Sarah forced a smile as she closed the door.

Dana turned around and saw that Angel Fire was missing. She called her name—no response. Neither down the stairs nor in the apartment, Angel Fire had gone MIA. She suspected that the cat might have escaped to 3A, and she rang the Medinas' doorbell.

Sarah's facial muscles tightened into a smile as she opened the door, and she said, "Well, hello again."

"Sarah, my cat Angel Fire was by my side a few minutes ago, but now she's missing. Have you seen her by any chance?"

Sarah shook her head no but said she could come in and check. Her friendly manner had a bit of a chill.

Dana followed Sarah through the Chinese-red foyer, its walls adorned with a photo gallery of children from around the world. Down the hallway, they heard purring from Emma's bedroom. Emma cradled the cat, and in return, the cat rubbed herself against her. Angel Fire usually showed affection only to Dana, so seeing the cat kiss the girl surprised her.

"Emma, honey, the cat belongs to Dana," said Sarah. "Angel Fire is a curious cat and she ran into our apartment to snoop around. Time to hand her back to her owner."

Emma refused. Her brown eyes watered as she hugged Angel Fire even tighter.

Dana said, "That's fine, Sarah. Emma can play with her whenever she wants. I guess Angel Fire is getting friendlier with people."

"That's very thoughtful of you, Dana. However, you know Emma has allergies."

Emma pleaded but reluctantly acquiesced to her mother's orders. However, the cat refused to come until Dana scooped her up.

Dana apologized, reiterating that Emma could play with Angel Fire at her place, or better yet, in the garden, and that she would make sure the interactions were brief. Sarah's expression softened, signaling that she approved of Dana's suggestion. Sarah intended to tell Manny about the get-together. As far as she knew, the Medinas had nothing scheduled that day, and could come over at three. They exchanged goodbyes.

Dana left with Angel Fire and headed back to 3B, while Sarah locked the door and went back to the kitchen. Supper would be turkey meatball lasagna. Emma ran back to her room and pulled out a notebook from her desk drawer. She found her special pink pen and started to write about the most recent dream she'd had—the one of herself inside a casket, a woman named Allie, and a cat called Angel Fire.

*

On Saturday morning, Angel Fire leaped on Dana's bed, poking her in the shins. Even after nearly nine years, Dana couldn't get accustomed to her pet's schedule or her brazen commandeering of her bed. She tried to shoo her off the bed, but Angel Fire repeated the action, forcing Dana to get up.

Dana filled a tiny tray with chicken and left it by the kitchen entrance. Angel Fire ignored it and jumped up on the counter, ready to drink from the running faucet. Dana turned off the faucet and pulled her rambunctious cat off the counter. Angel Fire decided to behave and ate the food in her tray. Dana quickly ran to her room and locked the door, hoping to get an extra hour of sleep. She succeeded in dozing off, until she was awakened by persistent scratching and whining. She opened the door, and Angel Fire scooted to Dana's bed.

"No, baby, no. Mommy needs her beauty rest," insisted Dana. "Be a good kitty and go to your corner."

She tossed a catnip toy onto the cat bed, but the cat refused to budge. Defeated, Dana hopped into bed next to the cat. Soon, they both fell asleep. However, Angel Fire repeated what she did at sun-up. The cat's eyes said more than her meows. Perturbed but patient, Dana surrendered. She had to forget about sleep, since the cat was hell-bent on micro-managing her time.

After her breakfast of coffee, orange juice, and oatmeal, Dana went about the business of being a hostess. She had bought the chocolate mousse cake and red velvet cupcakes the day before. The iced tea and lemonade containers sat in the fridge. She had already stacked up the paper plates and cups in the dining area. She emptied the taco and veggie chips into bowls.

Angel Fire started meowing non-stop. With the cat underfoot, Dana accidentally tripped over her, dropping the bowls filled with chips on the kitchen floor. She cursed as she tossed the scattered chips into the garbage. She would make do with the bag of potato chips left on the counter. Angel Fire continued to follow her—meowing.

Realizing that her cat probably wanted to be fed, Dana quickly opened a can of cat food. *That should shut her up*, she thought. She plopped the dish down near the cat before returning to kitchen duty. But the cat refused to eat. With her tail forming a semi-circle around her paws, Angel Fire quietly sat, staring at her mistress. Dana snapped, "Well, if you don't want to eat your breakfast, that's fine with me! As long as you mind your business, I can take care of mine, thank you."

She slapped together a mesclun salad with tomatoes, cucumbers, red and orange peppers, and red and green onions. She would cheat time by using her store-bought organic Italian dressing. She tried to slow down so that she wouldn't make a mess. Moroccan coriander was her special ingredient. When done, the salad could be kept in the fridge until her guests arrived.

After that, Dana began her pizza prep. While she drizzled extra-virgin olive oil on individual pita breads, Angel Fire jumped onto the counter. Dana shooed her off. Still meowing, the cat jumped back. This time, Dana grabbed the cat and put her in the bathroom off the foyer. With guests coming, she had no time to figure out what was wrong with Angel Fire.

By 2:45, the food chores were done, and she liberated Angel Fire from the bathroom.

Dana hurried for a last-minute hair and makeup check and a quick toilet break. Angel Fire returned to the kitchen to eat her food. Dana assumed that the cat, now silent, may have been nervous amid all of Dana's frantic preparations.

Sarah called and said that the Medinas would be fifteen minutes late. Ten minutes later, Jen called, apologizing that she was running late. She blamed it on the never-ending MTA weekend track work. Dana hung up and took a deep breath, not noticing Angel Fire circling around her legs.

*

Twenty-seven minutes later, the doorbell rang. Dana saw the Medinas through the peephole and unlocked the door. Sarah apologized for being late and Dana assured them it was no problem, ushering them into the living room, where they had snacks and beverages. Once seated, Dana said, "Sarah, can you tell me about the photos in your foyer? They're all so fascinating. Did Manny take them? A few of them look like they were washed in gray-blue. I couldn't really take a close look, because Angel Fire suddenly disappeared. I'd love to see them again. Some of the photos remind me of your drawings in *By Dave's Creek.*"

"Yes, Manny did get the inspiration from my drawings. Similar to what I saw in my dreams," answered Sarah.

Angel Fire dashed into the living room and sat by Dana's feet. The buzzer rang, and Jen Fein yelled into the speaker. Dana buzzed back and opened the door for Jen to come in. Both Dana and Sarah greeted her like an old college buddy. Jen handed Dana a bottle of Pinot Grigio and settled down on the sofa. Before the conversation resumed, Dana unscrewed the bottle and served the wine to her adult guests and poured chocolate milk for Emma.

"You know, Manny's more than just a smart techie," continued Sarah. "Being a photographer, he snapped photos throughout India, Spain, Italy, Greece, Egypt, Brazil, Kenya, and Indonesia. His work has been showcased at exhibitions worldwide. He has a show coming up at Rizzo's in SoHo this September. I'll keep you and Jen posted on the details. If you'd like to see the photos, please come over later."

"Yes, Sarah and I are both creative types," interjected Manny. "Glad she's finally doing what she always wanted to do—writing and drawing. She was laid off from Steinberger's in 2003. That was before this damn recession. Jen, you remember that horrible place? You were smart to get the hell out. Do you still work for *The New Yorker*?" His third beer took immediate effect.

"No, Manny, I told you I left long ago. I'm the senior editor for J. Coleman Publishing," replied Jen.

"Well, Sarah was never happy working in that hostile environment. She never got the respect she deserved. That bitch of a boss, Jill Myers, set the stage for the trouble that followed. Jill left for a cushy job at Focus NYC and her replacement,

Lance Walker, hated Sarah even more. He claimed it was the budget. Bullshit!"

Sarah poked Manny in the ribs. She whispered that he shouldn't be discussing this in front of Emma. She asked Dana if Emma could play with Angel Fire in the kitchen. Dana okayed her request, because Angel Fire, being one smart cat, usually didn't knock things over in the kitchen.

The conversation resumed, and Manny's face got redder as he spoke. "Tina, one of the art directors, related the news to Sarah that Lance Walker had hired a friend to fill her old position."

Sarah interrupted. "Mr. Beer-Belly Walker snooped around like a goddamn bloodhound. He caught me off guard when I was on the phone with Manny. Being on Jill's shit list made things worse, and he believed all her crap about my lack of leadership, anti-social tendencies, and not writing strong enough ads. He would attack my work at the weekly review meetings. He had a way of wearing down your self-esteem, speaking softly, with a subtle smile. His courtesies were reserved for those who fit "the brand"—the ones with better upbringings and sociable lifestyles. He had a vendetta to get rid of me. I couldn't fight the son of a bitch, since companies can ditch you for any reason under the No-Fault clause. After losing my job, and being three months pregnant, I moved in with Manny. I didn't believe in marriage, but Manny talked me into it for the baby's sake. During my pregnancy, I decided to write *By Dave's Creek,* which was loosely based on the Allie story. Job stress had made

194

it hard to concentrate on it, and I knew Allie was out to get me. If I didn't do it soon, I feared that I would also lose Manny and Emma."

Jen butted in. "And it helps to be married. The financial benefits are rewarding, especially with a surgeon." She saw the semi-sour expression on Dana's face, and said, "Well, marriage isn't for everyone. Sarah, it's great that you reassessed your life and became an author 24/7. You crashed the glass ceiling with *By Dave's Creek*. Those wild Allie dreams really inspired you. And at least you kept it clean." She took another sip of wine.

Jen continued. "It's amazing that you can do what you do and raise a kid. And didn't you tell me you like to have Emma critique your stories? She's an amazing child—inquisitive and imaginative, bright beyond her years. I'm infertile, but I'd rather stick to having a career than having kids. I wouldn't have the time for them."

She refilled her glass and shouted, "Hey, Dana, how the hell did you meet Allie? Are you writing the dreams down, like Sarah and Kate? I guess I'm not part of this secret society, never having met the brat. But I'd like to publish it whenever you ladies are ready." She finished her second glass of wine.

Dana excused herself in order to check on the pizzas. Minutes later, she brought out the Mexican pizzas on a Frida Kahlo plate and placed them on the glass-top coffee table. Angel Fire leaped on the table, knocked over the tray, and scattered the pizzas on the rug. Dana became distraught, and Sarah and

Manny picked up the ruined pizzas and brought them into the kitchen. Emma chased the cat into the bedroom, unnoticed.

In the bedroom, Angel Fire hopped onto the laptop. Emma whisked her off, and like a curious cat, she turned on the computer and waited impatiently for it to warm up. The icons finally popped up, and she clicked on the folder *The Allie Chronicles*. The Mac Office documents appeared by chapter, and her eyes popped like the icons. The story that she had been writing paralleled the version on the screen. When Sarah arrived by the doorway, Angel Fire jumped down. Emma read the second chapter until her mother took the laptop from her, shouting, "Emma, how could you!" Chills ran up and down Sarah's arms.

"Mommy, I'm sorry," cried Emma. "I followed Angel Fire. She jumped on the computer and meowed at me. She wanted me to look at *The Allie Chronicles*. We wrote about the same people. See?" Emma pointed to the screen for Sarah to look. "I have my notebook in my drawer as proof. Do you want to see it? I was having these dreams about Allie and Kate before we moved here."

"What? The Allie Chronicles? May I have a peek?" asked Jen as she marched toward the computer, finishing another glass of wine. Dana, with a quick nod from Sarah, escorted Jen to the living room.

"That's enough, Emma," scolded Sarah. "We're going home now." She faced her hostess and her husband, and said, "I'm so sorry for this. Manny, please take Emma home."

Emma tried to sneak out, but her mother caught her. She chided her daughter for not saying goodbye to Dana and Jen, and for not thanking Dana for her hospitality. Emma stuck her head in the doorway and yelled, "Bye-bye and thank you," and scooted out into the hallway. Jen managed to wave from the sofa.

Sarah said to Dana, "Kids! You try to teach them manners and they still do what they want to do. Dana, again, I'm sorry for all this trouble."

"Sarah, please. It's fine. I'll slice some of the chocolate mousse cake, and please take this box of red velvet cupcakes. The cake and cupcakes are from Melanie's on Seventh Avenue. I bet Emma would love them. How about some of the food I made; I hate to waste it. I'll give some to Jen when she sobers up. I plan to put her in a cab."

Sarah thanked her for putting the party together and said she would come back later for the food and cake. She apologized for Manny's and Emma's behavior. She also expressed concern about her daughter getting involved with the Allie dream-writes and asked if they could discuss it later. Dana understood her anguish and agreed to talk about it with her.

Sarah felt cold. The color from her face drained. "Dana, I must go, and yes, we should talk. I plan to sit down with Emma. This is more than uncanny. It's just plain weird."

Sarah hugged Dana and returned to 3A. Manny begged Sarah to forgive his big mouth, but Sarah didn't hear him.

197

Instead, she went to her daughter's room and asked Emma for her notebook.

Emma pulled out the pink notebook, labeled *The Allie Chronicles,* from her nightstand and handed it to her mother. Her dreams would no longer be her secret.

Sarah sat on the edge of her daughter's bed and read several pages. After several minutes, she closed the book, buried her head in her palms, and began to cry. Emma stood by her side and hugged her.

Chapter 19

Dana
(2010)

Jen had more than three glasses of wine. While everyone rushed into Dana's bedroom, she nursed a fourth, before making her grand entrance. After the Medinas left, Jen went back to the sofa and poured her fifth, feeling sheepish for her insensitivity.

Dana prevented the inebriated Jen from taking another sip and, worried that she wouldn't be able to make it home, insisted that she stay over for the night. Jen normally didn't overdo her drinking, and Dana suspected trouble in the Fein household. She asked her if something was wrong.

"I lied about Steven being in Chicago for a convention," admitted Jen, slurring her words. "He's cheating on me. He's already moved to the West Village with a girl half his age. I'm seeing a divorce lawyer next week. Dana, I'm so sorry that my personal shit messed up this party. Damn, I wasn't much help with the drama between Sarah and Emma!"

Dana commiserated with Jen before brewing a pot of coffee for two. While the coffee perked, Sarah called, and Dana invited her over. Sarah brought over a CD copy of the files and said she would be back tomorrow with Emma and her book. Dana poured coffee for Jen and herself; she hoped the caffeine would boost her energy and alleviate Jen's drunken state.

199

Between sips, Dana printed *The Allie Chronicles* from Kate's computer, as well as from Sarah's CD and her own version. She would ask Sarah to figure out how to tie everyone's story together. Meanwhile, she listened to Jen's promise to publish them in Kate's memory.

Angel Fire sat on her cat bed, watching intently, listening to the printer's continuous humming. She observed how Dana stacked the pages in three piles. When completed, Angel Fire followed Dana into the bed, next to the sleeping Jen. She jumped in between them, rolled over, and dozed off too.

*

Everything turned white in Dana's dream—the same dream that she had been having on and off since January. Snowflakes shaped like doilies made the sky and her surroundings white. Her black hair had been sprinkled in white frost, and the falling snow made her white cotton nightshirt and panties whiter. Snow melted on her face, leaving a refreshing and tingling sensation for a hot August dawn. But why was it snowing? Oddly, she wasn't cold. Something lurked in the distance. Heavy snowfall, now mixed with ash, hindered her vision. The blurry figure moved toward the forest, and Dana followed it. She ran barefoot, sinking deeper into the snow as she approached the outskirts of the forest. Everything looked dead, like skeleton sticks draped in pale gray. Even the fur trees had lost their evergreen. The snow thickened, yet the breeze remained pleasant. She wanted to go home, and her eyes opened.

The large snowflakes weren't snowflakes. They were pages from *The Allie Chronicles* blowing around the room. Dana had forgotten to shut the window. She placed the pages in numerical order, being careful not to awaken Jen or Angel Fire. This time, she placed the pages in three folders. For extra security, paperweights would sit on top of each folder. After that, bedtime, for some real sleep, she hoped. Jen and Angel Fire slept, peacefully unaware.

How peculiar that Allie, the adult, had run away from her. Was it because Allie had changed her mind about getting this story published, or that she feared that Dana would convince Sarah and Jen not to publish it?

*

At 3:05 a.m., Sarah lay awake, counting the seconds instead of sheep. Her husband's snores kept time like a metronome and he was unaware of his wife's insomnia.

She thought that, having found a man, she would be free from Allie, and Allie had, in fact, taken a long hiatus, giving her time to marry, have a daughter, and find a new career path. Sarah had kept her promise to Allie by sleeping with the deformed man, and enjoying it, and writing *By Dave's Creek.* Now Allie had come back as an adult, intending to snatch Emma from her. For two nights in a row she had dreamt of seeing her daughter in a casket, and Allie claiming to be her mother. Her daughter had the same dream and wrote about it in her journal, but seemed preternaturally calm about being in a casket. Had Allie poisoned her mind as revenge against Sarah for being married and becoming a mother? Sarah didn't think it had anything to do with putting the book together as a memorial to Kate. Or did it? She suspected that Kate's files might hold some clues.

Perhaps moving here eight months ago had been a mistake, but Emma had been insistent. Emma had run into Dana's duplex apartment, walking from room to room before setting herself upstairs in the small bedroom facing the backyard. This bedroom had been part of Kate Robbins's old apartment. Emma kept wailing, "Mommy, I'm at home here. I know this place; the lobby, the backyard." Emma had sat by the windowsill, mesmerized by the garden below. Dana's calico scampered in and hopped on Emma's lap. Dana ran upstairs to take the cat away. The cat was upset and cried. Emma sat on the floor, sobbing, and Manny had to drag her out of the apartment. The child protested loudly in the street, while Dana's cat wailed as if she were dying.

That dream tonight looked all too familiar, although the disturbing scenery nearly captured the essence of a Christmas card. She hadn't seen these woods for nine years. The evergreens looked barren from a recent fire, ashes mixed in with the heavy snowfall. She saw Dana running after an unidentified naked woman—then falling.

Sarah headed for the living room. Whenever insomnia struck, she would watch a movie from Netflix. She selected *Sleepless in Seattle. How apropos,* she thought. In went the CD. Seconds later, it ejected itself. She tried a few more times but got

202

the same result each time. She slammed the remote and cursed. She would watch NY1 on TV instead.

The reporter was talking about a three-alarm fire in the Kingsbridge section of the Bronx. Sarah watched her old apartment go up in flames—her bedroom and Allie's, the fire being confined to the corner apartment. The reporter noted that the resident, Mr. Thomas Quinn, an eighty-eight-year-old former janitor for P.S. 10 and St. John's Roman Catholic Church, was found dead in the bedroom. He had apparently fallen asleep while smoking in bed. The neighbors interviewed called him a gentle man who, sadly, had never married and had no family. *A man with a big heart, who cared for children and the homeless. He would do favors for people without asking anything in return. He went to St. John's Roman Catholic Church every Sunday and would greet you with a smile.*

Sarah clicked off the remote. She suspected that Mr. Quinn might have known Mr. Martin. They were about the same age, and came from the same background and religion, worked at the same places, and lived in the same neighborhood. Maybe Kate's old computer and her daughter's book would shed some light. She leaned back on the sofa and fell into a deep sleep.

*

At 7:35 a.m., a racket in the living room woke Sarah up. She didn't realize the time. "Oh, shit," she said, forgetting that she wasn't with Manny.

Emma ran past her mother and stared inquisitively at her disheveled appearance on the sofa. "Mommy, are you okay? You look like you were running in the woods."

Caught by surprise, she asked her daughter to repeat what she had said.

Emma sang, "Like Dana running in the woods chasing a naked lady. I saw her again in my dream last night. You have that same expression now, Mommy. Don't worry, it's only a dream."

Emma headed to the kitchen for a bowl of Cocoa Puffs. She yelled, "Mommy, slice me a banana for my cereal, please! We're supposed to be seeing Dana and the nice cat today, right Mommy? About my secret book and your secret files and Kate's and Dana's. Right, Mommy?"

"Emma, please tell me what you said about your dream. Mommy needs to know!"

*

After a fresh cup of coffee and a corn muffin, Dana and Jen waited for Sarah and Emma, but they didn't come at nine o'clock as scheduled. The doorbell rang a half hour later. Sarah apologized, claiming that they had both overslept. A refreshed Jen volunteered to assist Dana, Sarah, and Emma with the Allie project. Angel Fire followed them from the kitchen to the bedroom.

Jen turned on Kate's computer. Dana opened hers on her bed. Dana and Jen perused the different versions. Sarah and Kate's versions showed Allie's history. A common sex theme in all versions, starting with Sarah and ending with Kate. Yet Dana's version contained none of the above. She wrote only about her repetitive dream. Jen said it would work better as a novella than a short story, but that it needed a little extra spice and a storyline.

"You both saw me in the woods last night?" Dana asked Sarah and Emma.

Emma spoke first. "A naked auburn-haired lady named Allie ran in the snow and into the forest. Everything looked dead. Ashes were everywhere. She was still looking for her sweetheart, the deformed man named John Martin. Did you know that they're madly in love and want to have children together? But dead people can't have kids. The lady would like me to visit her more often and stay over for a while, because she needs me to help her find John. She's very nice, Mommy."

Sarah asked, "So you saw Allie, the same lady I saw in my last dream? Emma, please show us your book."

Sarah wondered if Allie wanted Emma dead as a way of adopting her. *How could Emma be so calm?* When the child suddenly refused to show the book because of a promise she had made a half hour ago, Sarah demanded to know to whom she had made that promise.

Emma evaded the question with a question. "Mommy, weren't you once John Martin's girlfriend? Well, sort of?"

"Sweetheart, you promised that you would show me the book again."

205

"Mommy, I really can't. I tore it up when I went into Dana's kitchen for some cookies and threw it in the garbage. The lady told me to do it before we left the house. She talks to me whenever I am alone."

"Emma, no!"

Dana dashed to the garbage pail, beating Emma by a few seconds. Jen followed. They both tore the pail apart, tossing last night's leftover pizzas, paper plates, soiled napkins, bottle caps, and fruit rinds on the floor. Sarah held her daughter at a safe distance. Dana yelled out for Scotch tape, while she and Jen feverishly pieced the pages together.

"It's in the top drawer to the left of the pantry," shouted Sarah, engaged in a battle of constraining her daughter—the daughter who hit and kicked her mother while begging everyone not to read her story, terrified that Allie would punish her for breaking her promise.

Jen found the dispenser and they finally pieced the pages together, the food damage being minimal. The story written in a child's hand held more information about Allie, Kate, and John than the adult versions.

Sarah felt relieved that Manny had left early this morning for a photo shoot in Long Island City and wouldn't be back until five. She couldn't fathom how he would have dealt with this paranormal situation. In order to avoid any further intervention or even violence by Allie, Emma was dragged into the laundry room next to the kitchen—the locked door, however, was not impervious to her uncontrollable crying and furious kicking and banging.

Minutes passed. The kicking and banging stopped and the crying faded. Dana and Jen finished the patch job. Both Sarah and she sat by the corner dinette, reading the story. Emma's version paralleled Sarah's and Kate's. However, the child's version shed more insight on the deformed creature, John Martin, and even Thomas Quinn, the man who had just died in the fire in that apartment in the Bronx. The story stunned them, its words and content way too mature to have been written by a child. Emma was precocious, but had she filled in as secretary to a ghostwriter?

Dana read:

The reclusive bachelors, John and Thomas, became best friends, even though John harbored revenge for his enemies, while the latter would give his last dollar to help a stranger. After John died during his arson attack on his mother, Thomas took his place as the janitor at P.S. 10. He remembered Allie from his friend's conversations over at his place. John always spoke of her fondly; in fact, he felt sorry for her. He and she had so much in common—they were both misunderstood loners. He pitied that black kid, Joey Coleman—an outsider like Allie. Unlike Allie, Joey stuck his nose in his books and became the top student in the class. John would talk to Allie about improving her grades and urged her to think about the future. Allie wanted to leave school and get married. John tried to discourage her. He'd tell her, "Get an education; prove that you can do it, like Joey.

Don't be a loser like me, a high school dropout from Hell's
Kitchen. Do you want to spend your days scrubbing toilets,
mopping floors, and living with your mother? Men with good
jobs want girls with an education. They want a girl who will give
them smart kids, not dummies without a high school diploma.
And college girls get nice office jobs and make better wives."

Jen interrupted. "Joey Coleman? You mean my boss, Joe
Coleman, of J. Coleman Publishing? He told me a few stories
about his early years at P.S. 10 and the dirty-water incident was
one of them. He sincerely regretted what he had done to Allie. I
recall reading about this in both Kate's and Sarah's versions."

Sarah said, "So this is not a coincidence? You work for
the kid who threw water at Allie?"

"I don't remember the girl's name or her description, but
that John Martin character sounded familiar," replied Jen. "Joe
said that if it hadn't been for this janitor's encouragement, his
life would have taken a different path."

Dana tapped her hand on the counter for them to stop
talking and let her read.

On Saturday night, John and Thomas would drink Pabst
Blue Ribbon and smoke Lucky Strikes. They played cards and
checkers. They'd talk about the good old days of TV—when TV
was black and white. Ernie Kovacs left more to the imagination
than crap like Rowan & Martin's Laugh-In. They'd debate about
The Tonight Show. According to John, Jack Paar was a better
host than Johnny Carson. Paar had smarter folks than all these

*actors and actresses. Thomas would jokingly disagree. Politics
became a battle of words . . .*

"Who gives a shit about Ernie Kovacs and political
history? Get to the real story, Dana," yelled Sarah.

"Jesus, Sarah, I'm trying my best. You try reading
Emma's scribbles."

Dana browsed the next pages before reading aloud:

*When it came to women, Thomas claimed it wasn't in the
cards for him. He broke his mother's heart when he became a
handyman instead of a priest. He was a janitor in several
apartment buildings along the Grand Concourse and moving
westward to Kingsbridge Heights, near Van Cortlandt Park, and
eventually to Kingsbridge, P.S. 10, and St. John's.*

Dana paused.

Sarah interrupted. "Dana, read on. I need to know where
all this comes from. It seems to jibe with Mr. Quinn, who died in
a fire yesterday; probably also with John Martin. See if you can
find anything else connected with Allie, besides her being pitied
by Mr. Martin."

Dana turned the page and continued reading:

*He wished his father, Sam, didn't die from the drink. It
only made his mother, Eileen, harder to deal with. He was the
only child after his sister's accident. When John was eight years
old, he and his five-year-old sister went to the bakery for bread.
Little Nola carried her doll, Maryanne, in her arms. After
purchasing day-old white bread, they hurried home. They lived
across the street from Houlihan's Bakery on Tenth Avenue. She*

dropped the doll while crossing the street. A truck swerved around and hit her. The driver claimed he never saw the auburn-haired girl. It all happened too fast. And there was little Nola, lying in the gutter holding her doll—broken and bloodstained. His angel sister was dead because of her doll, and his mother never forgave him. "It should have been you, Johnny, not her! You are like your father, bringing trouble into the house. You should both burn in hell." She'd beat Johnny for any transgression with his pappy's thick razor strap, before locking him in the basement. He would swear under his breath, "May the bitch burn in Hell." He wanted her to get a taste of Hell before checking in. But he didn't get his wish before he died.

Jen shouted, "This fits in with his cadaver-like appearance. Now get to the parts about Kate!"

Dana turned the page, which was stained with food and barely legible, and read it under the kitchen light:

He hated his mother so much that he saw a bit of her in every woman he met. But he loved me because I looked like Nola, and I was still a child. That was before Kate stole my man. They fell in love, and I could tell from the way they made love. I caught them leaving the forest after my transformation. I begged for him to stay. I begged him by asking Kate to stay and share our love together. I would do anything for John and saw it was possible for us to live together as a threesome. He liked the idea, but she said no. I pleaded to have him for the night, but she still said no. This time he refused her and gave me what I wanted. She was angry at first, but later joined in. I also asked John to

210

keep his monstrous appearance during sex. For some reason, I loved his damaged face, not his thick brown waves and bright eyes. We made love in perfect bliss. I cried when the pleasure ended and he left the forest with her. It's fine sharing sex with another, but I am more possessive. The forest was home and more beautiful than the world outside. I did forgive her and kissed her goodbye. But being alone in my beloved forest made me think of him and her—together. I saw the reflection of my womanly body in the pond and wept. Kate stole my man and now I'm alone. She will pay for her crime. She hurt me so much that I couldn't live in my lush paradise alone. I had to torch the forest. I watched it burn until the last ember died. The snow came to bury my world and myself. The gray-blue sky became gray-white, like the world I live in without my John.

"Goddamn Allie! That explains the snow-scene dreams," exclaimed Dana. "Now we know the reason why the forest is the way it is. But why do Sarah and I have these dreams? How come I'm the one, not Sarah, who's chasing that murderous bitch?"

"What about Emma?" shouted Sarah.

"Yes, if I can read these other pages," yelled Dana. "The food stains on them are making it difficult to read."

The pages fell out of her hands. The last two pages read:

Ms. Robbins is a thief. She stole my John. I wished for her death, and she went into cardiac arrest. John is not to know that I killed her. He still loves Ms. Robbins, and would hate me for my death wish. Ms. Robbins came back as Mrs. Medina's daughter, Emma. No one is to know this, although Mrs. Medina has an inkling from the way Emma has been reacting since they moved to Ms. Chu's building.

I forgave Ms. Robbins, because she reincarnated as Mrs. Medina's daughter. I always liked Mrs. Medina because she and I have a lot in common. Emma must behave and never show this little book to anyone. Regarding Ms. Robbins, I must keep my feelings hidden from John. And please make sure that my story gets written by Mrs. Medina and Ms. Chu, for Mrs. Fein to publish. I would like to be remembered in a memoir. I did not live long enough to become a writer like Mrs. Medina. My mother secretly wrote in her journal, and I inherited this trait from her. This is her story and mine.

By the way, Angel Fire was once my cat, Amber. Amber is living one of her nine lives as Angel Fire.

Love,

Allie

Suffer the lonely women for the sins of Eve. And the child who is writing this for me will sleep in a coffin tonight if my wishes are not kept by her.

Sarah's teeth clenched and she pushed Dana aside for a better look. She read aloud the last lines, which read like a biblical quote. The last line made her cry. She'd had that dream of Emma in a coffin. Why should her daughter suffer when she was innocent? Kate was innocent too. Dana was innocent. Even Jen, an outsider to the Allie dreams, was innocent, and whoever else preyed upon by that sinister girl and deformed man. It didn't matter who was worse. Not when Allie wanted to hurt Emma. She stammered as she told Dana and Jen about her nightmare.

Sarah went to the laundry room and unlocked the door. Emma sat on the floor with her back against the dryer—her eyes swollen, remorseful—her mouth open—gasping for breath.

"Mommy, I'm sorry. The mean lady instructed me to write all that ugly stuff in my book in secret. I would write whatever she would say in my thoughts. But while you were getting dressed this morning, the lady suddenly took my hand and wrote those last two pages. She said that I would die if I showed you my book." Her head was bent downward and her breathing was still erratic. She placed her hands on her chest and felt a horrible thumping inside.

Sarah fell to her knees. Face to face with her daughter, she cried, "What's wrong, Emma? Emma?"

Emma backed away into the corner by the sink. Wild strands of hair covered her face. Emma heard Allie's chant of *cat got your tongue?* over and over again in her head. Her heartbeat competed with her need for air. Her forehead broke out in a sweat and her pale olive complexion turned ashen. Emma fell over. Her heart wasn't strong enough to withstand the sudden attack.

Through the flap on the kitchen door, Angel Fire fled to the backyard. Sarah screamed out *why?* Dana couldn't answer. Jen called 9-1-1.

*

That night, Dana dreamed of an albino mouse hiding behind the washing machine, witnessing Emma's death. The crying made the mouse nervous. Unseen, she ran past them and out the cat flap on the kitchen door. The rhododendrons lay ahead. The mouse would rest and eat some of its leaves before sundown. The spirit that lived within the mouse had memories of living in a forest, and the gray-blue shadows of the leaves comforted her. The bushes came within view. The tired mouse, determined to reach its destination, grew more tired. Its pinkish eyes started to hurt—they couldn't tolerate the bright sunlight that had just torn through the clouds. The mouse slowed to a crawl, unaware of a hovering shadow. A loud thump followed, and the mouse couldn't escape—its neck was being ripped apart. It weakened quickly, losing to the strength and size of the shadow's owner. Nevertheless, the mouse wasn't eaten.

The cat, Angel Fire, killed the mouse out of revenge; Angel Fire saw Allie's spirit inside it. The cat spat out the mouse, leaving her to die on the brick walkway. Intense sunlight returned, and Angel Fire's shadow disappeared as clouds covered the Brooklyn skyline. Satisfied, Angel Fire purred, watching Allie's spirit fade like smoke.

Dana awakened and cried for Emma, Sarah, Kate, and herself.

Chapter 20

Dana
(2010–2011)

Shortly after the funeral, Sarah and Manny looked for another apartment, and by October, moved into the same brownstone in Boerum Hill that they had originally wanted. Sarah hated the thought of putting Emma's ashes in a cold mausoleum or in soil that turned to mud in the rain. She wanted her daughter nearby, interred in an urn in the master bedroom.

Sarah held the urn close to her and talked to it. She repeated this ritual every morning and night. Eight years old, and a sudden heart attack, probably brought on by shock. Emma's murmur had been considered insignificant, not enough to cause concern; even the doctors were baffled. Sarah still blamed herself for Emma's death, castigating herself for allowing the child to be locked up in Dana's laundry room.

Weeks passed and strange things happened at the new place. The photos of children hung lopsided. Sarah, who still kept in touch with Dana, mentioned it during a phone conversation. Sarah believed that Emma's spirit missed Angel Fire and that messing with the pictures was probably her way of reaching out for attention.

Dana offered to bring Angel Fire over later that night. Sarah agreed, and Dana arrived via taxi with Angel Fire, her cat bed, toys, toiletries, food, litter box, and scratching post. She heard construction going on in the apartment next to the Medinas.' A few weeks later, the renovations ended, and the problem with the picture frames was finally brought under control. Sarah knew that Emma must be happy to have Angel Fire around again. Shortly after, with Dana's blessing, Angel Fire became part of the Medina household.

Manny thought that having another child might help lift Sarah's depression, but Sarah did not want any more kids—she did not want to run the risk of losing another child. Manny suggested adoption. At first she said no, but later changed her mind. This happened before she learned that she was pregnant with identical twin girls. Slowly, she recovered, and wrote another children's book about baby animals, simply called *Babies*. Sarah's belly grew, and Angel Fire purred as she watched her pound the keyboard and draw the images. When it was finished, she dedicated the book: *To Emma, In Loving Memory, from Mommy.*

Katie and Amber were born in August 2011. Sarah had named the girls after her dead friend and her dead friend's cat. Jen promised to get *Babies* published by winter 2011.

Before taking on *The Allie Chronicles,* it would be up to Sarah to decide what to do about the manuscript. Dana asked Sarah for her permission to either take it or dump the files on Kate's computer.

Sarah choked up and told Dana to do what she wanted with them, but to please leave Emma out of it, to let her rest in

216

peace. Sarah had ditched her files after Emma died, and hadn't had any problems since she moved here. Sarah asked Dana to take the credit for writing the book, because she didn't want any part of it. She requested that Dana change her name and Kate's, and omit any reference to Emma. "Better still," she said, "throw out the files and printed sheets." Like Emma's book, she felt that the story should have been destroyed.

Dana promised that she would do it later that day. Yet she didn't inform Sarah about her endless nightmares of gasping for air while running in the snow. She figured, why talk about dreams when her friend was still grieving.

*

Joe Coleman liked eating at home. Not because it was cheaper, but because his wife, Melanie, had a reputation for being a superb cook. She could prepare heart-healthy, sugar-free, and low-sodium meals without scrimping on flavor. Joey thought she should have her own show on the Cooking Channel, to compete with Rachael Ray, with her own version of 30-Minute Meals.

Although the publishing field had taken a hit during the recession, Joe kept a positive outlook. He had struggled getting to where he was, and had suffered a tragedy, losing his wife, Laura, and their two sons, Carl and Curt, three years ago in a car crash involving a drunk driver. Mel came along a year later and became his angel of strength. Her birthday was a month away and he wanted to surprise his sassy Scorpion wife with an opal necklace from Tiffany's.

After dinner, Joe asked Melanie if she wanted to see the latest French film playing at Lincoln Plaza Cinemas, but she told him that she preferred to read a few chapters of a book she had bought yesterday. After Mel retired for the night, Joe took a peek at the book, which she had left on her nightstand. The name of the book was *Lori's Story,* and it was written by a new author, Anna Lee, a rising star on the New York literary scene. The book had gotten a decent enough review from *The New York Times.* He took it to his study. His normally cheerful disposition shattered as he read the first few chapters, and after a few hours, he slammed the book on his desk.

Joe had known the child protagonist when he was a kid, as well as the school, the assistant principal, and the janitor. He was that black kid who had thrown the water at the girl. All the names had, of course, been cleverly changed. Joe could not sue the author, who had a disclaimer at the beginning that any connections with those living and not living were purely coincidental. He had never discussed his early life with anyone at the publishing company he'd founded, except for his closest confidante, Jen Fein. *But why would she do this behind his back?* Faye Leonard had quit working as his executive assistant six months ago for personal reasons. Could she be the author? Her picture appeared nowhere on the book, but the name *Anna* could be from her middle name, Anne, and *Lee* could be derived from *Leonard.* Joe planned to discuss this with Jen in the morning. He threw the book into his attaché.

The next morning, Joe attended a meeting at the Citigroup Center on Third Avenue. After the meeting, he dropped by the Barnes & Noble before returning home. The store was gearing up for a book-signing event before Thanksgiving. He saw *Lori's Story* on display next to a sign in the window. The woman's picture on the sign was Faye Leonard's. His mouth tightened into a scowl. *Damn you, Faye, and damn you too, Jen!*

*

The next day, Joe arrived at the office before ten. He buzzed Jen and said, in a frosty voice, "Could you step in here for a few minutes? I want to talk to you about the author of *Lori's Story.*"

Before Jen could take a seat in his office, Joe tossed his copy of the book on the desk. "I'm the black kid who threw the water at the girl. Her name was Allie Harris, and the kind janitor was John Martin. How clever of you to feed our conversations to Faye, who conveniently quit six months ago, and how considerate of her to change the names. Were you aware that Faye, a/k/a Anna Lee, was planning to write a book?"

"Joe, I swear that I didn't have anything to do with Faye."

He shouted, "It's wrong to defame two innocent people I once knew. I had only respect for that janitor. He wasn't a racist. He used to encourage me: '*Study hard, Joey, and become somebody. Not like me, a high school drop-out.*' Why all the scathing crap and filth written against that poor girl, Allie, and

219

Mr. Martin! I eventually did apologize to the girl. It wasn't her fault that I was different, nor was it hers for being an outsider too. Her uncle killed her shortly after. I'll never forget her—never!"

Jen didn't tell him that Sarah had permitted Dana to do what she wanted with the *Allie* files. Or that Dana had decided against publishing the story and asked her to destroy the files, and that the files were dumped at home, not at work. Even if Dana had gone through with publication of the book, Jen would have edited out any information pertaining to Joey Coleman. But how could she argue with her boss against this bizarre coincidence? Realizing that her business relationship with Joe Coleman was now over, she resigned.

*

Three weeks later, Dana and Sarah skimmed through a few chapters of *Lori's Story* at the Barnes & Noble on Seventh Avenue in Park Slope. The similarities between this story and theirs amazed them. Dana looked at Sarah and said, "Why would Jen do this? I opted not to publish it and told her to destroy every version. She claimed that she did. She kept denying that she had confided in Faye Leonard, or should we say, Anna Lee. Well, we will never know the truth."

Jen had died in a car crash the previous month on the Jersey Turnpike en route to a family wedding. Her husband, Steven, survived the ordeal. They had not gone through with the divorce.

Dana thumbed through the book and exclaimed, "How clever of Faye to change everyone's names and a few places to protect her greedy ass."

Sarah added, "Oh yes, Faye was a first-class bitch when *By Dave's Creek* was being published. Jen claimed that Faye was a real snoop and could not be trusted. She would say, '*I don't understand why a decent man like Mr. Coleman would put up with her shit.*'"

They put the book back on the table display and exited before Ms. Lee was scheduled to arrive for her seven p.m. book event, thus avoiding a confrontation.

Anna saw Sarah Medina walking outside the bookstore. She said hello, but Sarah didn't hear her. Anna went inside with her publicist, George Braddock, and his editor friend, Bob Katz, from Bookender Press. Anna had to quit her job at J. Coleman's because she couldn't publish *Lori's Story* if she still worked there. She'd had the good fortune to meet George at a publicity party, several months prior. She used her charm to garner his attention and handed him her manuscript the following week. Through the right connections, her book had been published in September. Like a firestorm, it rose up the charts of *The New York Times* Best Seller List. She, Faye Leonard, now Anna Lee, was a literary celebrity.

She had her late grandmother, Deirdre Smith, to thank. Grandma DeeDee had told her about a journal given to her by an unmarried pregnant woman named Siobhan O'Neal, who had died in childbirth. The orphaned child was named Alexandra

221

Katherine, at Siobhan's request. After Grandma DeeDee died, Faye found the journal while cleaning out the attic. She grabbed the book and showed it to her mother. Her mom thought it was vulgar and insisted that it should be burned, but Faye saw dollar signs and took it to her one-bedroom condo on West End Avenue. Since Faye hated working at J. Coleman Publishing as Mr. Coleman's executive assistant, she decided to write the book and quit her job when the book went to press. In today's *Times,* she read that Mr. Coleman had suffered a fatal heart attack. He had recently retired from the publishing world and moved to Scottsdale, Arizona. She knew that Joe had a history of heart problems, hypertension, and diabetes. Faye thought to herself, *I guess death does come in threes—Jen Fein, Joe Coleman, and . .*

.

  The cameras snapped her picture. The flashing lights irritated her green eyes. Flame-haired Anna continued posing with her entourage and some of the neighborhood people who had turned out. She read portions from the book. She took frequent sips of water—the wine and the garlic sauce she'd had with dinner had made her mouth dry. With her nerves frazzled, she coughed a little but still managed to wow her fans. After the reading, people queued up for the privilege of having Anna's signature inside their books. Not accustomed to the spotlight, Anna became nervous. The previous week she had read at McNally Jackson Books and BookCourt. The following week she had book signings at Scribner's and Rizzoli's. Anna suspected that all this fanfare would eventually die down.

Something was bound to go wrong.

Her dreams of the forest covered in ashen snow told her so.

Chapter 21

Dana
(2012)

Dana dreamt about snow again. The flakes came down fast, mixed in with ash. The same figure she had seen in her previous dreams became clearer—naked and definitely female; her hair, medium length and dark auburn. Although athletic, Dana couldn't catch up to this agile woman. When she turned, Dana recognized her—Allie! The woman ran like a deer through the thickets, and soon Dana lost sight of her, blinded by the snow and ash. Chills gripped her and tension pounded her chest. She couldn't run anymore.

Dana woke up, gasping for air.

*

Sarah also had a dream. Not about the multiple shades of gray-blue or gray-white, the forest, Allie, Kate, or John, but of a hospital room. It looked dated, medicinal white, straight out of the '50s. She smelled the disinfectant, gauze, bandages, and blood—even rotting flesh. She saw a nurse walking toward a bed. A bed sheet covered the patient's head. She heard a woman's voice say:

"It should have been destroyed. I told the nurse, but she wouldn't listen. Instead, it was handed down to her grandchild. The grandchild would use it for her own self-interest and she

would be cursed. My daughter would cross the night path and walk into the dreams of lonely women who came in contact with her and write her story—they too would be cursed. Even their female friends involved with the story's publication—they would be cursed. Her story and my story would live on through them— they would be cursed. If any of these women had children, these children would be cursed. If they wished to rid themselves of the curse, the story, like that albino mouse at the warehouse, would have to be destroyed."

Sarah awakened on Saturday morning thinking it was just another stupid dream, like the one she'd had the night before. Her files got trashed after Emma died, as did the torn, food-stained pages of her daughter's little pink book, as well as Kate's and Dana's versions. Her children's book, *By Dave's Creek*, had been written as a harmless fairy tale, without any mention of sex, beatings, or rape. She tried to convince herself that she was immune to future trouble. *Did Faye open up a can of worms?*

Since she couldn't sleep, Sarah washed and got dressed, in baggy jeans and a raggedy gray T-shirt with a few holes in it. Since she was still breastfeeding the twins, she had thrown out her bras. Manny adored her fuller curves and found her leaking nipples to be ultra-sexy. Sarah associated long hair with the loss of Emma, and decided to stick with the super-short pixie she had gotten during her pregnancy with the twins. The areas around her forehead and eyes sported new lines. Like her silver strands, she had earned them. After Katie and Amber were born, she stopped

225

wearing makeup and donated her old clothes to local thrift shops. Her Manny loved her for her heart, not for her looks.

Angel Fire meowed for attention. Sarah shooed her away. The cat didn't listen and climbed onto the counter by the old portable radio; she used her paws in an attempt to turn it on. Sarah took the hint and turned it on, before slicing the strawberries into the Greek-style yogurt. She heard the usual—another sex scandal and killing in the City, and the never-ending political tension in the Eastern hemisphere. She drizzled organic honey over the yogurt mixture and added some flax for its Omega-3. While peeling a banana, the reporter mentioned a suicide over on the Upper West Side—*Anna Lee, the author of the runaway bestseller Lori's Story, was found dead from an overdose of prescription sleeping pills mixed with alcohol. An empty bottle was found next to her bed.*

Sarah thought about the dream and the woman's voice saying *it should have been destroyed,* that destroying it would free one from the curse. She suddenly thought of *The Allie Chronicles*. Maybe Dana hadn't destroyed all the printed copies and files. But that dream must be a warning that Dana was in danger. The curse had touched Kate, Emma, Jen, and now Faye. All of them had been involved in bringing the story to life through writing, and had died. She suspected that Joe Coleman's death had merely been coincidental, given that he was a male with health issues. She had to call Dana immediately.

Instinct demanded her to hurry. Angel Fire jumped off the counter and ran to her mistress's cordless phone on the

226

butcher block. She stood on her hind legs and meowed loudly. Her front paws pounded the cordless phone. Sarah pushed the cat aside and dialed Dana's number.

Angel Fire wailed in the background and jumped back on the counter. In the process, the yogurt bowl crashed.

Sarah's fingers tightened on the receiver. The busy signal became slower than her heartbeat, and the phone suddenly disconnected. She heard a siren a few blocks away.

*

Two days after Dana died of heart failure, Sarah found torn pages from Emma's book and bits of Dana's shredded version hidden in a rhododendron bush favored by Angel Fire, covered with rodent feces. She was not sure how they had gotten there but remembered seeing Angel Fire's body flash through the cat flap moments before Emma died, and she wondered which one it was—Angel Fire, a mouse, or a supernatural force—that had taken those pages to the bush.

After Sarah disposed of the pieces in the garbage can, she returned to the apartment and looked for Angel Fire. She called out her name, but the cat didn't respond. She didn't know that Angel Fire had slipped out of the garden, never to be seen again.

Epilogue

Siobhan, Angel Fire, and the Child (2012)

I, Siobhan O'Neal, wanted to commit suicide but changed my name instead. I tried taking an overdose of sleeping pills after the abortion more than fifty years ago. Good Catholic girls never played God with fetuses or with themselves. So I changed my name to Alexandra Nolan and lived, and had Siobhan die in my story. I intuitively knew the gender of my unborn child. Had I not had the abortion, the child would have been born a girl, and she would have been christened Alexandra Katherine. I went to confession a week later, and the priest forgave me, but I never could forgive myself for killing my unborn daughter.

Alex stopped typing and blew a smoke ring from her cigarette. She cleared her parched throat with Madeira wine, her mind still lost in reflection.

I went back to night school at City College and kept my dream journal by the nightstand. I typed the stories of Allie's world on my Smith Corona. After several typing and sales jobs, I, Alexandra, better known as Alex, found a secretarial position at Cooper and Smith Advertising. Through hard work and perseverance, I moved into the more lucrative copywriting position. After several years, I became one of the senior writers.

228

However, office politics, my lifestyle, gender, and age prevented me from going further.

Alex continued pounding the keyboard—pounding out her commentary while her thoughts pounded in her head:

I was and still am a loner by nature. John Martin, a handyman from Fordham Road in the Bronx, fathered my child, and the bastard refused to marry me. I could never let another man touch me because I still harbored love for him. I created events based on Allie's fictitious life, family, and thoughts, as well as John, whom I portrayed as the deformed, sex-crazed yet desirable creature. Brent was the opposite—charming, handsome, and successful—the man you read about in fairy tales and saw in movies but could never attract in real life. The child, Allie, was a composite of myself and what my unborn daughter would have been like. Emma was the daughter I could never have. Sarah and Kate were microcosms of myself, even though Sarah got married, became a published author, and found some happiness in her life. Dana turned into the person I wanted to be. Jen came from an unattainable world of branding and retouched sales pitches. My on-the-job experiences with women and men gave my story additional credence. Instead of killing myself, I killed off my characters. However, I decided to keep Sarah alive. Like me, she lived to remember her loss.

When computers replaced typewriters, I updated the story as I witnessed the changing world, yet was afraid to publish it. Although a work of fiction, I felt that I still needed to protect my privacy.

229

Alex took another sip and thought:

Ever since Cooper and Smith Advertising forced me out back in 1999, I started painting scenes from my dreams. Gray-blue forests and exotic flora predominated the canvases. The most striking ones are those of a burning tree. The leafless tree bled, burned without being consumed. The tree represented 'Siobhan'—a burning reminder of what John did to me. Like my story, I keep the significance of my paintings private.

Alex stored her twelve paintings in the walk-in closet. Number thirteen hung on the wall by her desk. She resumed typing and stopped when her glass became empty. She poured more wine and lit another cigarette. She thought:

But I need to publish this book for additional income. The recession has tightened my budget. The stock market ate up most of my savings. Six dollars and change sits inside an old red leather wallet. I, like my wallet, have seen better days. Still, I have to smoke at least a pack of cigarettes a day and drink a little wine—my venial sins. I keep telling myself that these sins haven't killed me yet.

Alex looked down. Her one-eyed cat sat by her feet, looking up at her mistress.

I've always loved cats, especially calicos. In the story, I used the names of all the cats I've owned—Chloe, Ginger Snap, Amber, and Angel Fire. Angel Fire is my current pet. She watched me type my fifth rewrite. Poor thing! Since that attack, I'm keeping her inside. Alex gently hugged Angel Fire. The burns on the cat's left side, as well as the area by the damaged eye socket, had been healing nicely.

Upon completion, Alex took another drag from her cigarette and finished her wine. She sat for a few moments, reflecting on her accomplishment. Her manuscript was finally ready.

Angel Fire meowed, and her pixie-haired mistress asked her, *"What's the matter?"* The cat stared at a moving object in the kitchen and ran to the pantry. After several minutes, Angel Fire gave up on a potential meal. She sat, meowing to be fed.

Alex went to the pantry to get the cat food; however, when she opened the door, the shelf was almost empty. Alex had forgotten to buy extra cat food. She usually went to the local bodega because it tended to be cheaper than the other places, thanks to the damn hipsters who had ruined her neighborhood. She knew doom would hit her affordable neighborhood when the Fresh Direct trucks started making their daily visits. She wondered how much longer she would be able to stay in her small rent-controlled apartment in Long Island City. She heard rumors of the building going co-op and new ones sprouting up on vacant lots. After drinking three glasses of wine, she became too sleepy to buy the cat food, and went to bed instead.

She left the window by her desk open, with full trust that Angel Fire would not escape again. Unfortunately, the heat wave had been costing her money, and she had to cut back on her A/C consumption. The window faced a backyard that had two maple trees. The trees provided some shade to cool off her top-floor apartment.

Angel Fire climbed onto the desk and walked across the keyboard, pushing the manuscript toward the ashtray. She saw an albino mouse chewing on a cord behind the computer and pounced on it. While her fangs ripped its neck, one of the pages touched the lit cigarette left in the ashtray—the cigarette slowly toasted the edge until it ignited. Soon the rest of the pile caught fire. Angel Fire dropped the mouse onto the keyboard and fled out the open window. She hesitated, then made a dramatic leap to one of the tree's branches and climbed down. The mouse wasn't as fortunate. Weakened from its wounds, it couldn't outrun the advancing flames. The fire spread to the computer and leapt upward to the painting of the burning tree—this time the tree was consumed by the fire. Alex woke up, entrapped, and the apartment was engulfed in flames when the firefighters arrived. Soon her life was deleted, along with her story in words and paint, and the albino mouse.

The firefighters contained the fire and were able to spare the adjacent apartment from too much damage.

*

Frightened by the oncoming traffic, Angel Fire waited until it was safe to cross. Instinct told her to keep going. A copper-colored tomcat followed her. Fear told her to keep going, faster than before. Fear walked alongside of her, as she remembered how the evil man had tortured her outside the building, and now, the apartment fire. She would have been

232

burnt to death if she ran back to warn her mistress. Humans came into view, and the leering tom retreated. From one unfamiliar neighborhood to another, Angel Fire took naps and ate scraps, but she was still hungry and thirsty. An open trashcan had leftover chicken wings in a broken cardboard container. The approaching dark made her nervous. She hated being outside whenever it turned dark or light. It reminded her of the attack. She quickly ate what she could and continued uptown.

She got to a place where a few cats were eating from pans on top of a stoop. Angel Fire ran up the stairs. The smell of tuna and chicken tempted her. The local cats hissed at her attempts to squeeze through. One tuxedo queen growled and chased Angel Fire down the steps. She waited until the group finished before eating. Only a few morsels remained in the bowls. Angel Fire licked the bowls clean and drank the remaining water. A woman opened her screen door and brought out fresh bowls of chicken giblets and water. Out of gratitude, Angel Fire purred and bumped her head against the woman's legs several times. She stood on her hind legs, wanting attention, wanting help.

Although the cat wasn't wearing an ID tag, the woman could tell by her behavior that the one-eyed calico was not feral. The cat appeared to be recovering from recent injuries. The woman planned to take the cat, whom she called *Patches,* to a no-kill shelter in Manhattan.

At the shelter, the vet checked Patches for a microchip ID underneath the skin between her shoulder blades and found

233

nothing. She gave the cat a thorough examination and determined that she was basically healthy, albeit dehydrated.

*

A month passed, and one day a man brought his granddaughter to the shelter. She had originally wanted a dog for her birthday but now wanted a kitty. Her eyes scanned the cages and she heard a young cat meowing. She fell in love with Patches and pleaded for Grandpa Charlie Harris to let her have the cat. He couldn't resist spoiling his only grandchild and answered *yes*. They brought the cat home in a cab to one of the new luxury condos along River Terrace in TriBeCa. They drove through the inner courtyard, past the azalea and rhododendron bushes, to the entrance.

On her birthday, she smiled for Daddy's iPhone video, holding her happy cat on her lap. She sat on her green and pink butterfly bedspread. The walls were painted sunshine yellow. According to Daddy, the room had been designed for a princess. However, she insisted on keeping a cage housed with two white mice from her science project. She named them *Dana* and *Jen*. Dressed in a new blue and white gingham dress, she embraced her cat, whispering, "Don't worry, Angel Fire, you will never be hurt again."

She renamed her *Angel Fire* because it was the first thought that came to her when she first saw the cat. The cat reminded her of Amber, the calico from her dreams, and her beloved pet, Emma. She still wrote about Amber and herself in a secret journal she hid in her nightstand. Later that night, she read an excerpt to Angel Fire:

Amber lives in a magical talking tree near a pond in a beautiful forest filled with sunshine and exotic flowers. An evil man comes and changes everything. The pond turns muddy and smells rotten. All light and foliage are tinted in gray-blue. He puts white mice under a spell to perform wicked tasks. He threatens to abduct the princess from her palace outside the forest. He hates Amber and wants to burn her in the talking tree.

In real life, the ten-year-old princess had red hair, chubby cheeks, and depression. Her older sister, Nola, had died a year and a half ago. A drunk driver plowed into The Artisan Sweet Shoppe on Pacific Street in Brooklyn, killing Nola as she crossed the street, holding a chocolate fudge cupcake for her sister. The princess blamed herself, as well as the bullies at school, for the tragedy.

The princess would have to undergo more reconstructive surgery for burns on her face and arms from a fire last year in their dove-gray Park Slope brownstone on Garfield Street. The au pair had accidentally left the window open. A breeze blew the café curtain toward the lit scented candle and ignited the curtain. The child tried to stop the flames, and in doing so, was badly burned. The au pair's quick response saved the child's life. However, the child's cat, Emma, who had been hiding under the bed, was burnt to death.

The unfortunate princess's name was Allie, named after her late mother, Alexandra Sarah Katherine Kahn-MacDonald,

235

the *Cinderella* wife of Brent MacDonald, the CEO of M.D. Securities. Her mother had been sexually assaulted at knifepoint and stabbed in the chest five times. Due to exsanguination, the medical staff couldn't save her, but they were able to save her premature baby by emergency C-section. They thought it was miraculous for little Allie to have survived.

According to the latest reports, her mother's assailant is still at large.

About the Author:

Patricia Carragon is known throughout New York City as an energetic and indefatigable writer/poet/curator who runs the long-running and popular Brownstone Poets Reading Series in Brooklyn Heights, New York. She is also an emerging photographer.

Ms. Carragon has been widely published in journals (both online and in print) and anthologies, including *A Gathering of the Tribes, Alien Buddha Press, Bear Creek Haiku, BigCityLit, The Café Review, Concrete Mist Press, First Literary Review-East, Indolent Books, Jerry Jazz Musician, Live Mag!, Muddy River Poetry Review, Narrative Northeast, The New Verse News, Nixes Mate, Panoplyzine, Poetrybay, Oddball Magazine, Orbis International Literary Journal, Sensitive Skin, Silver Birch Press, Stardust Haiku,* et al. Her poem "Paris the Beautiful" won Poem of the Week from *great weather for MEDIA*. She has work forthcoming in the *Paterson Literary Review* and *EOAGH*.

She is also an avid performer of her work in various venues throughout NYC and its environs.

Recent publications include her first book of fiction, *The Cupcake Chronicles* (Poets Wear Prada, 2017) and a haiku/photography chapbook on cats, *Meowku* (Poets Wear Prada, 2019). Other books of poetry include *Innocence* (Finishing Line Press, 2017), *Urban Haiku and More* (Fierce Grace Press, 2010), and *Journey to the Center of My Mind* (Rogue Scholars Press, 2005).

In addition, she is an executive editor for *Home Planet News Online*.

She lives and creates in Brooklyn, New York.

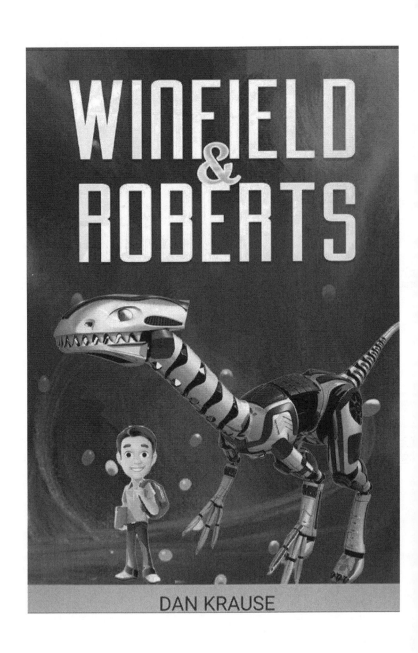

DAN KRAUSE

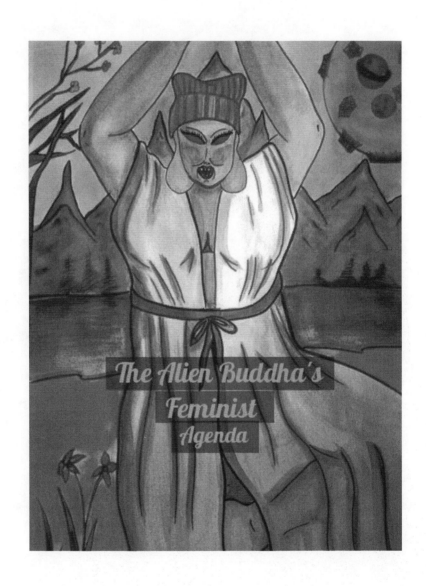

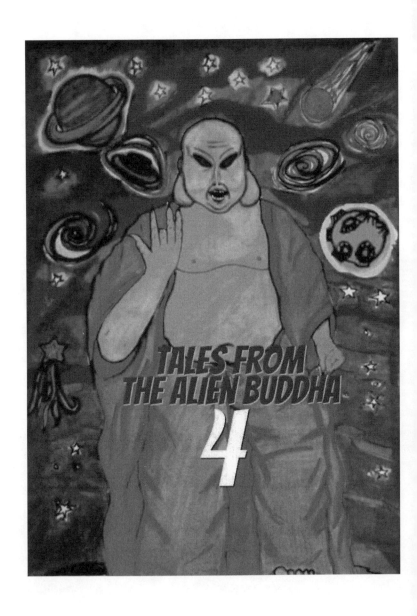

RED FOCKS

A Gruntled Folk Artist's
Disgruntled Folk Art